A Spy Worth Saving

Book 4 in The Seductive Spies Series

By
Cheri Champagne

Jacket design and illustrations by Deana Holmes
Editing by Jen Graybeal, Beth Attwood, and Amanda Bidnall

ISBN: 978-1-7777443-6-6

Dedication

For everyone with a natural inclination to help others.

A Spy Worth Saving

Prologue

London, May 1815

A low fog rolled over the cobblestoned street and up Hugh Haddington's trouser leg, the chilled moisture causing gooseflesh to break out over his skin. The moon was only slightly discernable through the thin layer of clouds and smog that marred the dark London sky, but it told him that it was well past the midnight hour. To Hugh, however, the night was still young.

He breathed deeply of the cool, humid air swirling around him, the familiar odours of coal, horses, rot, and fetid water assailing his nostrils.

Anticipation rolled through him as he observed his quarry, following at a discreet distance. The man wore shiny black leather shoes, a billowing greatcoat, and a tall hat. He swung a walking stick—that Hugh assumed hid a thin blade of some kind—at his side.

The clipped footfalls of his target echoed off the close buildings of Cheapside. A cat hissed in the darkness somewhere off to his right, but Hugh set his gaze unwaveringly forward.

The man himself hadn't drawn the interest of Hugh's superiors, but he had been a close acquaintance of the Marquess of Grenewood—a man known to have committed countless treasonous acts. Hugh had been given the assignment out of an abundance of precaution. That was until Hugh had begun to tail the bastard. As of that evening, he had proof of the man's guilt, and he could scarcely wait to report it to his superior. Another of Napoleon Bonaparte's spies taken down.

With a swift glance about, Hugh's quarry turned sharply onto an adjoining street. Hugh reached the corner and put his back to the wall, keeping to the shadows, before peering around the corner.

His quarry entered a bawdy establishment. Hugh smiled, his zeal for an evening of combined work and pleasure sending tingles of eagerness up his spine.

He trod on silent feet to the establishment's entrance and pulled the door open. Candlelight flooded the small section of cobblestoned street, the drunken laughter, high-pitched crooning, and awkward notes of an ill-tuned piano spilling out through the door. He stepped over the threshold and immediately spotted his quarry with a voluptuous brunette lightskirt already sitting on his lap.

The establishment was as flagrantly wicked as one could expect from a bawdy house. The walls, floors, and furniture were draped in stained and torn red fabric—the actual material was unknown to Hugh, and likely the men who frequented the house cared not for fine trappings—while nude paintings and statues graced the walls and every surface of the room. The air was hazy with cigar smoke and heavy with the scent of sex and perfume.

Delighted at his luck, Hugh situated himself upon an armchair not far from his target and accepted a cheap brandy from a woman walking by.

While he did not ordinarily frequent bawdy houses, it had been far too long since he had tupped a woman. He had a preference for widows as bed companions, as they required finesse and the reward was far greater. But in a pinch, a whore would do well, indeed.

Swallowing his brandy in one burning gulp, he reached for a woman passing by, his fingertips caressing the skin of her forearm. "Beggin' your pardon, love…"

With a saucy smile, the whore guessed at his intent and sat across his lap. Hugh nuzzled her perfumed neck, and a refreshed brandy appeared in his hand. He tossed the liquid back with a squeeze to the whore's arse. She giggled and rubbed her exposed breasts against his brown tweed waistcoat.

Once his quarry retreated to the rooms abovestairs, Hugh would do the same. He wrapped his arms around the lightskirt as his gaze flicked upward toward his target.

Then he stilled. His quarry's seat was empty. His hold still on the whore, Hugh eyed the other bawdy house patrons, searching for the familiar face. *Ballocks! He's gone!* Instinct quickly took over. Without a second thought, Hugh lifted the half-nude woman from his lap and stood.

"Damnation," he grumbled as his vision blurred. He took three steps and faltered with another curse. *I've been poisoned,* his inner voice warned. Somehow he had blown his cover and alerted his quarry to his pursuit.

Despite himself, his pulse began to race—likely an effect of the poison. What had he been given? How much time did he have?

The room spun around him as he staggered toward the door. Where had his drink come from? Who had prepared it? He tripped over the edge of a low table and tumbled forward, the air rushing from his lungs with a winded *oof.* Cursing again, Hugh rose and dashed clumsily forward, reaching for the door as the doorman pulled it open.

Laughter and lewd remarks filled the room behind him, and though Hugh couldn't quite discern their comments, he knew that he'd caused a scene. It mattered not; his only concern was to flee this place before his quarry returned.

He flung himself through the door, nearly toppling over in the process. He breathed deep of the familiar scents carried on the cool, damp night air, hoping they would help him to regain his senses.

Blinking through his blurred vision, he strode forward, his drugged clumsiness making his footfalls no longer silent, but loud and uneven.

"Ballocks," he slurred.

If Hugh could but make it two streets down, his younger brother, Philip, had a goldsmith shop that might very well be his salvation.

Swift footfalls approached from behind him, and Hugh's gut churned. He withdrew a pistol from its holster within his coat and spun toward his pursuer.

"*You,*" Hugh growled. He was tempted to ask the man how he knew that Hugh was following him, but he already knew the answer. Hugh had slipped up. He was losing his touch, and he ought to be ashamed.

"You are a fool, Hugh Horace Hebert Haddington."

Hugh cringed at the sound of his full name. "I might be a fool, but *you* are a traitor," he sneered. "You deserve to hang from the end of a rope." He oughtn't be so forthright, but he would likely die soon, and one ought not leave this world with a lie on his lips.

His quarry growled and withdrew a thin blade from his walking stick.

A laugh split the air, and Hugh realized belatedly that it had come from him. "I knew you had a blade in there!" he crowed, slurring as he pointed at the weapon.

The man swung his miniature rapier through the air, the whoosh making Hugh's head spin faster. Hugh aimed his pistol and pulled the trigger. *Bang!* The weight of the shot threw Hugh off balance, and he staggered backward.

His opponent froze long enough to take stock of his person, then laughed. "You dunce!" He guffawed. "You missed me."

All at once, the man was upon him. Hugh tried to block his quarry's blows and jabs, but, Lord help him, he couldn't bloody well *focus*. The man's taunts were punctuated by the fresh sting of his wounds.

Spots began to float before Hugh's eyes, and laughter and vile insults filled his ears as the pull of unconsciousness tempted him.

The last thing he heard was the resounding *thwack* of his face hitting the cobblestones.

* * *

"Ah, good then! He's awake," a voice said.

Hugh blinked, but his vision was still dark. He lifted a hand to touch what he was certain was a large knot on his head when something stopped him. The dreadful rattle of chains and the intense pressure of manacles around his wrists held him in place. He was sitting on a damned floor!

"What the devil?" His voice was muffled, and he realized all at once that a sack had been placed over his head. *How?* His memory flooded back, and dread settled heavily in his stomach.

Achingly familiar laughter surrounded him. Hugh knew that voice, and he knew what it meant. But he couldn't accept defeat. He'd freed himself from dire situations before; surely he could once again.

With a sudden burst of hope, Hugh thrashed, pulling at the manacles on his wrists and ankles—and his sodding neck. The metal bit into his flesh, and the fresh tang of iron in the air told him that he'd cut himself. *Hell.*

"Do not try to struggle, Haddington," the voice drawled. "There is nowhere to go, even if you *should* escape."

There had to be hope of escape. There *had to*. The drug had left Hugh's system; surely if he could see and locate something with which to pick the locks of his manacles, he could find a way free of this place. Beyond the scent of perfume and his own blood, he could smell… Hugh took a deep breath through his nose. *Greenery.* He was near to the out of doors, for certain.

"How long have I been unconscious?" Hugh asked, interested to learn how far out of London they'd driven.

His answer was blinding pain as his captor struck him hard across the face. Spots formed behind his eyelids, but Hugh shook them off.

"*I* will ask the questions, Haddington!" He heard the man take a step to the side. "What is the name of your superior?"

Hugh's blood chilled. "I'm afraid I do not comprehend your meaning."

A hoarse shout was pulled from his lungs as a sharp blade sliced through the tender flesh at his waist. Warm blood trickled down his skin.

"I will ask you again," the voice whispered into his ear. "What is the name of your superior?"

Hugh took a quivering breath, then ground out, "Do you mean at the mill?"

Crack! With a clean sideways snap, the man broke Hugh's little finger, eliciting a roar of pain from Hugh's chest.

His captor gripped Hugh's hair through the sack and pulled his head back to hiss in his ear. "I know who you are, Haddington. I know that you've been following me for some time. What I don't know, however, is the name of your superior.

"I have an endless amount of time to question you. I can assure you that my collection of weaponry is extensive, as is my imagination and"—he sniffed the side of Hugh's head—"my *zeal* for torture. I will happily wait for your response to my questions…but if you do not answer, I promise to keep you living long after you have begged for death."

In that moment, Hugh abandoned all hope of ever escaping with his life.

Chapter 1

Tilting her face up to the treetops, Charlotte Bexley smiled into the lightly falling rain as she walked her mare through the dense forest around her neighbour's estate. Lord Reddington was rarely at home, and was in possession of a splendid orchard that Charlotte availed herself of at every opportunity. The orchard was just beyond the edge of the forest, and while it was still early in the year, they'd had an unseasonably warm spring, and she had hopes that there would be some budding fruit. If there wasn't, then she would hunt for rabbits on the return ride home.

Leela trotted happily between the trees, her hooves cracking old sticks and branches with each step.

"Good girl," Charlotte murmured.

She spied a narrow path to her left, and led Leela toward it. A change of scenery would be just the thing.

Five minutes down the path, Charlotte's stomach growled. The rain was coming steadily now, the sky above the treetops a light grey. She had packaged herself a lunch, but she was loath to sit in the rain to eat. If she were to find fruit in the orchard, she would satisfy her hunger with that, but surely the sandwiches in her saddlebags would be ruined in this weather.

Nudging Leela faster, they traversed the gradually narrowing path of the forest, the overhanging trees becoming closer, their long, outstretching branches nearly touching Charlotte's lilac bonnet and the bow slung over her shoulder.

"This is getting perilous, is it not, Leela?" Charlotte crooned to the mare as she drew them to a stop. She slid from the saddle, landing on the forest floor with a soggy *squelch*. "I cannot risk breaking one of your legs simply because I chose a different path."

Carefully, Charlotte led the mare through the forest. The *pitter-pat* of rain hitting the leaves echoed around them, and peace settled over her at the comforting sound.

She scanned their surroundings, searching for any sign of the path's end, when something caught her eye. A small wooden structure, no wider than her arm's length, sat hidden among some shrubbery. It was small, but it would be an ideal place to eat her lunch and enjoy a brief respite.

Her stomach growled in response, and with a mirthless smile, she led Leela forward. The trees grew increasingly dense as they neared the structure.

"This is close enough, Leela." Charlotte patted the horse's shoulder.

She quickly tied the mare's reins off on the branch of a nearby tree. Adjusting the bow and quiver over her wet shoulder, Charlotte retrieved the satchel of foodstuffs from the saddlebags and strode toward the little structure. The wood was dark and beginning to curve upward at the edges from rot and moisture. It was poorly constructed but, remarkably, still standing—though leaning ever so slightly to one side.

The door's latch was missing the lever, but with a hard tug it swung out toward her. Charlotte's senses were immediately assaulted by an amalgamation of unholy odours coming from within the small space. With a wheezing cough, she pinched her nose against the scents of bile, urine, blood, rot…and death.

Squinting into the darkness as her eyes adjusted, she spotted a dark mass upon the structure's floor. She stifled a gasp. Some poor animal had been trapped inside! She crouched in the entry, one hand on the door's frame for balance as she attempted to get a better look at the poor beastie.

A low groan emanated from it, and Charlotte leapt back before promptly losing her balance and falling to her bottom on the wet forest floor. Pain jolted through her, but the sensation was quickly replaced by fear. Her heart fluttering wildly in her chest, she scrambled to her feet and reached for her bow and quiver, aiming the arrow at the structure's entrance.

When an animal attack was not forthcoming, Charlotte slowly and cautiously approached. A faint *clinking* and *rattling* of chains echoed from the small space, and Charlotte frowned. Was something held *captive* inside?

She returned to her position in the doorway, the faint quivering of the chains indicating that the creature was trembling. A wave of compassion swept through her and she returned the arrow to her quiver and draped the bow across her back.

"Shh, shh," she hushed. "There is no need to be afraid."

The creature had retreated to one corner of the diminutive space, and Charlotte squinted at it through the darkness. A sudden and alarming sense of recognition shook her and she gasped, choking on the virulent stench.

"*You're a man!*" she exclaimed.

* * *

Hugh's hands trembled as he held them in front of his face, blocking the painfully bright grey light beyond hell's entry. The shackles at his wrists pulled against him, rattling in protest at his movements.

"It is all right," the soft, lilting voice said. "I will help you."

His curst hope scented the air, but Hugh tamped it down. Any hope had died long ago, along with his pride, self-respect, and courage. Weak and frail, he had nothing with which to fight back, to protect himself. And even if he had, what did he care any longer?

There was shuffling, and Hugh pressed himself further into the corner, his ever-present pain throbbing through him.

"Please," the crooning voice said. "Have some water."

Hugh peered over the edge of his hands at the woman. She was a shadowy blur, the bright, grey light from beyond the door frame creating a halo of light around her. His heart gave a hard thump in his chest. *She is an angel.*

Rain rattled the roof of his prison, the water dripping through the cracks to land rhythmically on the wooden slats of the floor.

"Drink," the angel urged, lifting a leather pouch to his lips.

If his captors had sent this woman to kill him, surely they would have found someone more bloodthirsty to complete the task? No, the man who had imprisoned him wanted Hugh to languish until he was either ready to reveal his secrets or he was dead. They'd kept him fed and watered, but only enough to keep him alive.

If the woman were here to poison him, however, would this not be an adequate means to ensure that he consumed it? But no. His captor would undoubtedly wish to witness his death; he would not send someone in his stead.

Hugh eyed the woman with gradually subsiding suspicion for several heartbeats before he accepted the pouch of water. He raised it to his cracked and bleeding lips and drank greedily, the fresh liquid dribbling over his chin and down his neck as he gulped.

"Easy, now," the angel said. "If you drink too quickly, you will get yourself sick."

It was too late for that.

"*Please*," he croaked. "Help me."

She shuffled forward, her expression betraying nary a bit of the disgust she must have felt in this hell of a prison.

"Of course," she whispered. "But you are chained. How am I to free you without the key? Shall I fetch a rock to break the chains?"

He gestured weakly to her shoulder. "Your quiver." His voice was gruff but faint. "May I use an arrow?"

Without a word, The Angel obliged, retrieving an arrow from her quiver and handing it to him. His fingers fumbled, and his lungs laboured with even those small movements, but he managed to thread the tip of the arrowhead into the keyhole of his left wrist manacle and twist.

The rain fell harder, the droplets now a steady roar on Hell's roof. Streams of water dribbled to the floor, pooling with the waste around his chains.

Unbidden, a groan of frustration and defeat escaped him. He felt the resistance of the lock, but couldn't push past it. A month, chained to the floor without sufficient food and water, had significantly weakened his muscles.

"May I help?" The Angel asked.

Hugh nodded, dropping his hands to his lap. The Angel took the arrow and gently cradled his wrist in her palm. Her skin was warm and clean; guilt twisted his stomach at the thought of soiling her.

"Are you able to guide me?"

"Yes," Hugh whispered, his breathing laboured. "Put the tip…of the arrow inside…and angle it outward. Now…turn it counter-clockwise…until you reach resistance."

He could feel her movements before she stopped.

"Good," he urged, licking his cracked and bleeding lips. "Push."

The *click* of the lock opening was loud to Hugh's ears, despite the drone of rain above them. The Angel removed the manacle from his wrist, and suddenly he felt lighter of heart, the weight of the past month slowly beginning to lift.

He tried to smile at her, but he doubtless had the appearance of a feral animal snarling. "You did…wonderfully."

Hugh closed his eyes as The Angel moved on to his second wrist and then to the manacles around his neck and ankles. Soon, he was free of his chains, the burden of his imprisonment lifted from him. Despite himself, tears flowed heedlessly down his cheeks, and a faint sob was wrenched from his throat.

The Angel clasped his hand in hers, her compassion tangible even in her touch. "Come," she begged. "We must be away from this place."

Indeed. He had no notion of time while in Hell, and the villains tasked with keeping him alive could return at any moment.

With difficulty, The Angel helped him rise to his unsteady feet. His body shook perilously, his legs wobbling. His joints *cracked* and *popped* as he moved, and his aches and improperly healed wounds pulsed with every rapid beat of his heart.

Her unquestionable reservations aside, The Angel slid under his arm and wrapped hers about his waist, letting him lean his weight upon her shoulders as she helped him out of perdition.

Fresh rain charged them from above, the cool water dripping down his forehead and dampening the threadbare material at his shoulders. Gooseflesh rose on his skin. It was wonderful.

"My horse is just there," she said, gesturing ahead of them.

Hugh lost his balance and stumbled, but The Angel held his weight. "Thank you," he mumbled.

She *tsked.* "Do not thank me yet. You are gravely injured and malnourished, and may yet perish. We must—"

A loud ringing sounded in Hugh's ears, cutting off The Angel's words. Dizziness swiftly followed, the forest spinning around him.

"I'm afraid I might faint," he confessed.

The Angel held the burden of his weight heavier on her shoulders as they neared her mount.

"Not yet, you don't! You must get on the horse first, for I'll not be able to lift you."

Hugh's feet dragged with each step, the earth muddy beneath broken twigs and close shrubbery. Trees were all around them, just wide enough apart for them to get through without turning sideways.

They came upon The Angel's mount, a handsome coffee-brown mare with large white spots. The beast side-stepped away from them, her eyes warily watching Hugh. The Angel helped Hugh to lean against a tree before she calmed her mount.

"Shh, shh," she hushed in the precise way that she had done for him. "There, there, Leela. We will do what we can to help this man, you—"

"Hugh," he grunted.

The Angel spun to face him. "Pardon?"

"My name…is Hugh."

Ringing filled his ears once more, drowning out her response. The tree abraded his back, and he quickly realized that he was sliding down its trunk. The Angel rushed to his side, holding him upward as he righted himself on his feet. They walked to the horse's side, and The Angel kept him steady as he lifted his foot into the stirrup. The pommel was wet and slick, but his hand was big enough to wrap around it as he awkwardly—and with help—lifted enough to drape himself across the saddle on his stomach.

"I…cannot go…further," he admitted with a twist to his gut.

The Angel put a hand to his stinging back. "That is well enough, Hugh. We will get you to safety."

His eyes grew heavy as they slowly began to move. The beast's gentle motion jostled him, and he groaned.

Hugh did not know where they were going, and he did not particularly care, for only one thing truly mattered to him now: he was *free*.

Chapter 2

Charlotte kept a hand to Hugh's back as they drew to a stop at the rear of her home an hour and a half later. The rain continued to pour, soaking through their attire. She might be chilled, but the flush of excitement and fear rushing through her body kept her warm.

Hugh had long since lost consciousness, the poor, sickly man. Her curiosity about his circumstance was piqued, to be sure, but she would not inquire until he had regained his health; there was no sense in paining him further.

How odd that she'd found the man on Lord Reddington's land. Despite being a powerful landowner in the area, her neighbour had not made himself available to the residents of Leicester, preferring to keep to himself while here. But surely the man wasn't capable of *that*; he was a lord of the realm, for pity's sake, a man who voted in Parliament! Perhaps some other blackguard had found the hidden location and decided it an ideal location for their captive.

Her mind reeled. What if someone had put Hugh there in the hopes that they could use the poor man to somehow punish Lord Reddington? But why choose *Hugh*? Could someone among his staff be capable of such a despicable act?

She shook her head. Whatever the reason, and whoever was responsible, she knew that no man deserved to be treated as Hugh had been. She could never regret her decision to take him in.

A sigh escaped her as she shook her mind free of her turbulent thoughts.

As much as she might wish to bring the man directly indoors to doctor him, she must clean him first. His odour was so foul that tears sprang to her eyes at its sharpness. It was impossible to assess him through the layers of filth, and while the rain might have soaked him through, it had done little to actually clean him. The man had been left to die in his own excrement, for heaven's sake.

"Stay here, Leela." She patted the horse's neck and withdrew to the stables.

It was a small wooden building that contained enough room for two horse stalls, a carriage, a cart, and a feed and tack room. Charlotte's sodden skirts slopped with every movement as she traversed the small space. Gathering the necessary items, Charlotte placed them on the cart and wheeled them over to Leela and Hugh.

"*Drat,*" she whispered with feeling.

Pondering her task, she placed her hands upon her hips and eyed the man and the cart. She didn't want to hurt him, but she hadn't a choice but to move him. Lord knew what injuries he had incurred; what if she aggravated something?

With a sigh and a tumultuous swirling of nerves in her stomach, she carefully slid Hugh backward off the mare and laid him onto the cart. She gently rested his head on the wooden rim of the cart, his matted and filthy shoulder-length hair hanging over its edge.

Charlotte dashed to the water pump, filled a pail to the top, then returned to the man's side.

"If you can hear me, Hugh," she said soothingly, "I am going to wash your hair."

She'd found her husband's—Lord rest him—sandalwood-scented soap in the storage room, and rubbed a piece between her wet palms. She created a lather and spread it through Hugh's hair. When the foam grew grey and thick, she rinsed it with some of the water, then repeated the wash. It took several tries before the soap washed away clean.

Next was his attire.

"Your hair is clean," she told him. "Now I must remove your ruined clothes and clean your body. It is necessary, I'm afraid, in order for me to assess your injuries."

She pulled a pair of shears from her pile of items, and began to cut away his tattered clothes. As the layers were removed, she saw just how thin and damaged the man was. His bones jutted out under his sagging skin; she could count his ribs, as his broad ribcage was put in stark relief. She held back a gasp as she noted the scars and bruises on his person. He had unquestionably broken bones that had set improperly. But as much as she wanted to care for his wounds, she had to get him cleaned and inside before he caught the fever. Heavens, even a cold might kill him in his current state of frailty.

Careful to keep herself detached and her curiosity unappeased, she slid his filthy clothes—with the exception of his drawers—from beneath him. She lathered the sandalwood soap on a cloth and quickly scrubbed him down. Charlotte was comforted by the pinkening of his pale skin as she cleaned; at least he had enough blood in his body to create a flushed response. With difficulty, she rolled him to one side and cleaned his back, then quickly did his other side, dipping her cloth in the water with each pass.

When the skin that she had exposed was washed to her satisfaction, Charlotte knew that there was one more place she must clean. But Lord knew she couldn't touch him *there*.

Retrieving the shears, she cut his drawers, then averted her gaze as she drew the material away. With a deep breath and a grunt, Charlotte lifted the pail of soapy water and dumped it over his nether region.

Hugh groaned, a deep frown marring his clean brow.

"My apologies, Hugh. This shall all be over soon."

Charlotte gathered her last item—one of her husband's nightshirts—and crouched at Hugh's side.

"I know this is terribly inconvenient, but I require your aid, Hugh." She put one arm beneath his shoulders and urged him upward. "Please sit up."

His eyes were still closed, but he complied. Carefully, Charlotte fit the nightshirt over his wet head and guided his arms into his sleeves. She tugged the material down his body so as to provide a modicum of privacy.

Charlotte helped Hugh back into a reclined position then swiped at the rivulets of water trailing down her temples. In the interest of speed, she lifted the end of the wagon and dragged Hugh to the rear door of her modest home.

The building had three floors and spanned only three rooms on each side. The brick façade appeared bright red on sunny days, but through the rain it was a murky rust colour. The back door's white paint was chipped and peeling with age. Charlotte put the wagon down in front of it.

Rounding the wagon, she tugged open the door, then slipped her hand into Hugh's limp one. His nightshirt was already soaked through, gooseflesh spreading across his pale skin.

"Come, Hugh. Stand with me."

He groaned, and Charlotte tightened her hold on his hand.

"By my troth, I will support you all the way," she assured him.

* * *

The whistle of wind through a tight space and the rattle of rain on a window wove their way into Hugh's consciousness.

His body felt heavy, each limb nigh impossible to move. He slowly opened his eyes, his lids dry and rough. The room was dim, the deep-blue window dressings lending the room a cerulean hue that mingled with the flickering of a low-burning fire. Without lifting his head, he could scarcely determine the room's layout, but it was of moderate size and comfort. And he was most certainly lying upon a bed.

Whose bed? he wondered.

While he was grateful to be free, Hugh hadn't the foggiest notion of where he was or how he'd gotten there. Someone had taken great care to ensure his comfort, however, for he wore nightclothes—though damp—his skin no longer itched, and a warming pan had been placed beneath the counterpane by his feet.

His entire person throbbed in time with the beat of his heart: his muscles, his bones, the scarcely healed wounds that had not been tended and were likely beginning to fester. He ached fiercely. Hugh held on to that pain—embraced it—for as much as he might be grateful for his release from hell, he'd certainly deserved to perish there.

Wind rattled the window and gently fluttered the window's dressings. The sound was closely followed by a series of rapid thumps from the floor above him. Hugh stared at the ceiling, his brow lowered in a puzzled frown. *What the devil?*

A soft knock sounded at the door to his left before it crept open, bringing with it light from the corridor beyond. And immediately, Hugh's memories came flooding back. *The Angel saved me.*

"Oh!" She stopped mid-stride, a tray laden with dishes rattling in her hands. "You're awake!"

Hugh's heart squeezed at the sight of her. He hadn't seen her clearly before, but now he took her in. Her hair was the colour of freshly brewed coffee, wet, slightly curling, and half-fallen from her coiffure. She had matching slender eyebrows arched high above her sharp and curious grey-blue eyes. Her lips were full, rosy, and curved upward in the corners, and her nose was straight and narrow, which perfectly suited her heart-shaped face and strong jaw. Even from his prostrate vantage point, he could see the abundance of freckles peppered over her skin. He'd never before found freckles particularly attractive, but on The Angel they quite took his breath away.

His gaze travelled lower to her practical attire. She wore a serviceable green paisley morning dress with long sleeves and a white apron overtop, clearly a change from what she'd worn while rescuing him.

Suddenly aware that he was staring, and that The Angel was waiting for his answer, Hugh cleared his throat, wincing at the painful response. "Yes," he croaked. "I am awake."

She strode toward his bedside and placed the tray on a nearby table. "And how do you feel?"

"Sore…and tired." His voice was low and hoarse. "I am alive and free, however, for which I must thank you."

Her face lit up, her smile broadening to show her straight white teeth and her eyes crinkling fetchingly in the corners. Hugh's heart flipped over.

Damnation. Have a care, man, he reminded himself. He didn't even know the bloody woman, and his body had decided that she was his. How had she found him? What relationship did she have with sodding Reddington? Could this be a part of his torture—to show him care and offer him hope, only to rip it away? Hell, even if she *was* innocent, just his being in her home was putting her in danger.

There was no denying, however, that he required help. So while he would accept it graciously, he must keep his heart and hope firmly reserved.

"You are most welcome." She clasped her hands in front of her. "I do hope that you don't mind, but I've brought a poultice and bandages for your wounds."

She eyed him with hesitation, a rosy hue creeping across her chest and up her neck. Hugh vaguely recalled her perfunctory bathing of him, and almost laughed. He had lived the last month in his own excrement; the least of his current concerns would be modesty and pride. Besides, having a pretty woman touch his skin was a far sight more appealing than the abuse he had become accustomed to. If she *was* in league with Reddington, he would die in comfort at the very least.

"I have no objection to your doctoring," he rumbled. "In fact, it would be much appreciated. I give you leave to do as you please."

The Angel smiled, and Hugh's heart squeezed once more. Damn this reaction to her!

Hugh's eyelids grew heavy, and he gave in to the desire to close them. The dishes *clinked* as The Angel moved about. The curious mixture of lavender and sandalwood permeated the air, and something inside him rejoiced. It had been too damned long since he'd smelled something other than rot and shit, and the feeling was both maudlin and joyful.

Then her hands were on him.

She lifted the bedclothes, pulling them down past his feet where she began her examination. Hugh knew not if she was trained in the art of doctoring, or if she merely had practice bandaging wounds, but her gentle touch and soft clucking at his injuries was comforting.

Keeping his eyes closed, Hugh listened to the gentle *pitter-pat* of the rain against the bedchamber window, the *clinking* of dishes, and The Angel's soft breathing as she examined his person and bandaged his wounds.

* * *

After careful assessment, Charlotte came to the conclusion that Hugh did not have any critical injuries; however, several of his bones had been broken and improperly set, he suffered from severe malnourishment, and he was in dire need of rest and proper care.

Her heart panged with pity and sorrow, as it had all through her examination and treatment. His entire body was covered in healed or healing lacerations and what she could only assume were the scars from bullet holes, burns, and stab wounds. One of his ears was missing a chunk out of the lobe, and his neck, wrists, and ankles were raw and festering from his imprisonment. It would seem that his captors had made the effort to keep him just alive enough to continue his torture.

In any other circumstance, Charlotte would choose to call upon a doctor to break and reset Hugh's bones and care for his wounds, but the local physician worked under Lord Reddington, and while it was entirely possible that some other blackguard had put Hugh there, she had a bone-deep feeling that Reddington was somehow entangled in Hugh's treatment. Reddington and his staff mightn't be aware of her occasional pilfering of his fruit and game, but surely someone among his staff would have noticed the little building, and the unfortunate man within. And if they had found the little building, would they not have informed his lordship? It didn't seem possible for the man to be completely unaware of Hugh's presence, and for that reason, Charlotte had decidedly *not* summoned the physician.

While she had set broken bones before, she had never done so on a man so large and in need of correct handling.

Chewing on her bottom lip, she brought the bedclothes up to Hugh's waist and stood back in thought. One of his little fingers was crooked to one side; the angle at which it currently sat would likely impede any use of his hand. His left shoulder felt out of joint. She could easily return it to its socket, but she knew not how long it had been dislocated, and it could cause a great deal of pain to the poor man to reset it.

Her gaze travelled over his pale face. His facial hair was long, wiry, and peppered with silver. Hugh's dark blond, shoulder-length hair had a slight wave and was still damp at the ends from his washing. And his eyes… Charlotte almost sighed aloud. His eyes were forest-green and seemed to penetrate through to her very soul.

"Have you concluded?" Hugh's rough voice danced along her spine and sent fluttering waves of *something* through her abdomen, and she cursed the feeling. The poor man had likely either lost his voice from lack of use…or from too much screaming. Either way, it was shameful for her to enjoy his raspiness.

She forced a smile and said truthfully, "I'm afraid that I have come to an impasse." Hugh watched her expectantly, and she continued. "You have several bones that have been broken and set improperly, and while most will not impede your movement, your finger and your shoulder require readjustment. I hesitate to summon a physician, as he would undoubtedly reveal your presence in my home and, based on your circumstance, I assume that would be unwise."

If it was possible, his face seemed to pale further.

"Most assuredly," he confirmed.

"I am able to set them," she hastened to say. "I merely worry about the pain it might cause."

Hugh slowly shook his head, his hair rubbing against his pillow. "I can assure you, the pain that setting my bones might cause is naught when compared to…" He paused, then pressed his lips together, apparently unwilling to continue.

She knew what he was going to say, of course, and she would have to agree: torture was likely worse than what she had to do. It didn't sit well, however, that she would have to inflict pain.

With a sigh, Charlotte nodded her understanding. "Very well."

Prolonging the action would only increase the nerves rattling around her stomach, so without preamble, Charlotte cradled Hugh's hand in hers and clasped his little finger.

"Breathe in," she said warningly.

He inhaled.

Crack!

Chapter 3

Beef-scented steam rose from the pot and clung to Charlotte's face as she stirred it. Her stomach growled, and she smiled ruefully. She would get her share once Hugh had eaten. He must be famished.

Turning from the large cooking fireplace to the tall table in the centre of her kitchens, she cupped a handful of chopped vegetables and slid them into the pot. Her spices were on a tall shelf to the right of the fireplace; she selected several bottles and returned to the pot. She added a generous helping of the spices and stirred the mixture together before returning the spices to their spot on the shelf.

Her kitchens were the pride of her home. Every other room was small, but cozy. The kitchens, however, were grand for a home that size. One wall was dedicated to the large cooking fireplace, with two ovens to one side for her baking and shelves for her spices. On the left wall were large windows that allowed her bright daylight over her washing bins. On the wall opposite the fireplace was a long table used for wrapping the cured meats that she smoked in her smoke house, which sat just beyond the kitchen gardens. To the right side of the kitchens were the doorways to the larder, scullery, and another door that led into the hall. Along the wall was a long cabinet that housed dishes, glasses, goblets, and cutlery, and near that was the table where they took their meals. Above the tall worktable in the centre of the kitchens was where her pots and pans hung for convenience and accessibility. The space was organized precisely how she preferred it.

Bright grey light filled the room, and a pleasing hum drummed against the window as rain fell outside. With another stir to the pot, Charlotte sighed happily and turned back to the table.

Light, quickly paced footsteps approached from the hall, and she smiled to herself.

"*Boo!*" a small voice cried.

Charlotte spun in mock horror, a hand to her chest as she feigned surprise. "My goodness! You frightened me!"

The little cherub-faced boy laughed with glee as he bounced on his toes. "I scared you, Mama!"

Charlotte laughed at the little four-year-old. "You did, indeed, Maximus."

"Mama, Mama!" another voice called.

Dusting her hands together, Charlotte accepted a hug from her seven-year-old son, rubbing her hands through brown hair that matched her own. "How do you fare, Quintin?"

"Very well, Mama," he replied.

Maximus bounced, his light blond hair flopping about and his brown eyes alight with youthful curiosity. "Who is the man, Mama?"

"I am not entirely sure, but his—" Charlotte began.

"Did he *die*?" Max interrupted.

"No, he—"

"We heard the screaming, Mama," Quin said. "It was very loud."

Max gasped, then screeched, "Did you *kill* him?"

"Is he a pirate?" Quin interjected. "He was hairy like a pirate."

Maximus jubilantly cheered. "Ooh! Pirates! Where did you find him?"

"What if he washed ashore after a battle with—"

Charlotte clapped her hands together, the loud *crack* stiffening her sons' spines as they drew alert and watched her intently. "I can say with a modicum of certainty that he is *not* a pirate. And I did not kill him, for pity's sake. He is abovestairs, recovering from his injuries."

"What happened to him?" Quin asked.

Max nodded. "How did he get injured?"

"Will he sleep in your bed with you?"

"What's his name?"

"When will supper be prepared?" Quin's gaze slid past her toward the pot of soup.

"I'm thirsty!" Max announced loudly.

Quin scratched at his chin. "May I have a biscuit?"

"Manners, boys!" Charlotte admonished. Her head was veritably spinning with the number of inquiries.

"We apologize, Mama," they mumbled in unison.

"If you both wash your hands, I will set food and water on the table, and you may have a biscuit then."

Max jumped with his fists in the air. "Huzzah!"

Both boys ran toward the doorway, then shoved at each other so that they might reach the doorway first.

"No pushing!" Charlotte called.

"Sorry, Mama!" they shouted from down the corridor.

With a deep sigh, Charlotte returned her attention to the beef and vegetable soup boiling over the fire. She tested the stiffness of a carrot with the edge of her wooden spoon and found it perfectly cooked. Retrieving two thick cloths, Charlotte lifted the pot from the fire and placed it upon the worktable. She gathered four bowls and ladled soup into each, then found the buns that she had made that morning and placed them on separate plates.

Max and Quin dashed into the room just as she set the bowls on the table.

"That seemed rather quick," she noted. "Did you use soap?"

"Yes, Mama," they said in unison.

Charlotte pursed her lips and gestured toward their hands. "Let me smell."

Quin held his hands out, but Max watched the floor.

"Maximus?" She raised an eyebrow at her youngest son.

"I forgot," he confessed.

Charlotte clucked her tongue. "Off you go to wash your hands properly." She wouldn't spend their precious funds on such a costly luxury if she didn't think it necessary. She'd even resorted to purchasing them soap with a citrus fragrance just for their use. If only her sons would *use* it.

"Yes, Mama." He darted away.

"You may eat, Quin," Charlotte said as she put the biscuits on the table and her son sat at his favoured spot. "I must bring some soup up to our guest, so I will put you in charge of ensuring the dishes are placed in the washbasin."

Quin nodded, his cheeks rounded with his bite of crunchy biscuit. With a quick buss to his forehead, Charlotte filled a dulled silver tray with the necessary items and strode purposefully toward her bedchamber. She would have given Hugh a different room, but hers was the only available bed that would fit a grown man.

Pirates and growling stomachs aside, her sons had asked rather pertinent questions. Where *would* she sleep? It would be improper— even for a widow—to sleep in the same bedchamber as a man who was not her husband, most particularly when her children were at home. She would have little choice but to sleep in the unoccupied servants' quarters, or on the settee in the morning room.

Once upon a time her home had been well staffed, but now every duty fell to her and Mrs. Laurie. The kindly woman, however, lived with her husband a half of a mile away and only came to assist Charlotte out of the goodness of her heart.

She sighed as a thought occurred to her: she would need to write to Mrs. Laurie to request that she not lend her aid for the coming weeks while Hugh was in residence. Perish the thought if the woman discovered a man in Charlotte's bed and created a scandal among the neighbours or brought Lord Reddington's wrath to her door.

Charlotte ascended the home's main staircase to the second floor.

While inquiries regarding her sleeping arrangements were indeed excellent questions, two others were prominent in Charlotte's mind: *Who is Hugh, and what happened to him?*

* * *

Hugh stared dazedly at the ceiling as pain pulsed through his body. His thoughts grew increasingly foggy with each breath, the weight of his failures and the relief of potential freedom fighting for control over his emotions.

He squeezed his eyes shut as his mind played over the events of that fateful evening—as it had done every night of his imprisonment.

What had he done to expose himself? His footsteps had been silent, and he was certain that his quarry hadn't spotted him. Did his quarry have a partner that Hugh hadn't seen? Hugh had never revealed his name to his captors, but what if they'd had him followed in return, and learned it on their own? Were his brother and his brother's family safe?

A soft knock sounded at the door before it crept open. Hugh did not have to open his eyes to know that The Angel had entered. He was vaguely aware of her approaching footsteps and the sound of clinking cutlery.

His eyes still closed, Hugh opened his mouth to utter a greeting, but only a hoarse growl came out.

"Hush now." The Angel's soothing whisper sent warmth swirling around his chest. "I have prepared soup. Are you able to eat, or would you prefer to wait?"

A low, warning grumble rose up from his stomach, and he huffed a pained, wry breath. With effort, Hugh opened his dry, bleary eyes and licked his cracked lips. "I wish to eat," he whispered, his voice hoarse, "but I…lack strength…"

The Angel nodded, a lock of her coffee-coloured hair falling over her freckled brow and one grey-blue eye. "I will help you."

Hugh watched as The Angel retrieved the tray and placed it upon the opposite side of the bed. She then settled her hip on the edge and slid her arm beneath his neck and shoulders, carefully cradling him as she reached for a spoon and dipped it in the broth.

Her body was warm against his, her full breasts pressed against his shoulder. He would be hard-pressed to resist arousal if he wasn't so weak. At the moment, however, it was a great comfort just to have someone touch him without inflicting pain.

She spooned some beef and vegetable soup into his mouth, and he drank greedily, the savoury, spicy flavour making him salivate between each spoonful. His stomach filled quickly, but he was still anxious for more.

The Angel returned his head to his pillow, and Hugh almost groaned.

She clucked her tongue. "You must eat slowly; if you overfill your stomach, your body will reject it and your recovery will take longer. I will bring a buttered crumpet in an hour."

As much as he desired more of the delectable soup, he knew that she was correct, and he was grateful that he had his very own angel watching out for him.

"Sleep," The Angel advised.

Hugh closed his eyes, and images of his capture instantly appeared in his mind's eye. A low growl rumbled in his chest, and a frown creased his brow.

"For whom do you work?" Hugh's captor demanded.

Hugh coughed, blood spilling over his split lip and down his chin. "I work for Mr. Knight at the cotton mill. He can attest to—"

"Enough!" the man spat. He slashed his hunting knife though the air and cut deeply into Hugh's chest. "Tell me!"

A cool hand touched Hugh's forehead, and he flinched.

"Shh, shh," his Angel hushed. "Go to sleep."

She slowly caressed his forehead, stroking from between his eyebrows to his hairline in an agreeable, repetitive motion. Calm settled over him, and his tense muscles gradually relaxed until, at last, he slipped into sleep.

* * *

Charlotte waited until Hugh's breathing deepened before she withdrew her hand. His skin, while scarred, was smooth, and pleasing to touch. Something about the wounded man plucked at the strings of her heart. There was a visceral need to help him within her. She wished that she knew more about him, knew where he was from, what he enjoyed, and how he came to be in that little structure hidden deep in the forest. But despite that desire, she wouldn't press him; the man had been through enough.

With a softly uttered sigh, Charlotte stood and gathered the tray. On silent feet she quit the room, stepping into the dimly lit hallway and closing the door behind her.

"Boo!" Maximus cried, leaping out in front of her.

Charlotte yelped and jumped, her tray and dishes rattling.

"I scared you, Mama!"

"Indeed you did, Max." Releasing a long breath, she continued down the hall and noted Quin joining them from his position against the wall.

"Did you learn anything about the man?" Quintin asked animatedly.

Charlotte shook her head. "I should say not; it would be rude to inquire. He will volunteer information if, and when, he desires. The man cannot even lift his head, he is so bone-weary! We must allow him to rest." She eyed her sons with a raised brow. "Do you understand? You are to leave Mr. Hugh alone."

"Yes, Mama," the boys said in unison.

They traversed the short hall and descended the main staircase to the diminutive foyer. The brick walls were enclosed in plaster, their bottom half covered in white-painted wood panelling and the upper half decorated with green-and-blue-striped floral paper. The interior of the home had been designed by Mr. Bexley's aunt—who had owned the home before Charlotte's husband had purchased it—and while the style was dated, Charlotte had always found it rather cheerful.

Their footfalls echoed along the walls as they made their way to the darkened kitchens. She placed the tray on the worktable and spun toward her boys.

"I am going to eat my supper and wash the dishes. *You*"—she pointed at them—"are to march to your bedchambers, put on your nightclothes, and brush your teeth." Charlotte mightn't be able to afford full-time staff, but she would unquestionably spare the expense for tooth powder. "Is that understood?"

The boys nodded and dashed away.

Charlotte quickly ate her meal, then set herself to the task of washing the dishes. She looked up at the darkness through the kitchen's window, but saw only her reflection staring back at her. Once upon a time she'd lived in a lavish home with countless maids and footmen, two cooks, a butler, and a housekeeper. They'd perform these tasks—and many others—so that she wouldn't have to soil her hands.

Lifting her hands from the soapy dishwater, Charlotte examined them. They were worn and callused, chapped and freckled from the sun. But she could not regret the decisions that brought her to where she was. Her sons were the joy of her life, and Charlotte would not exchange their existence for any amount of hired help, jewels, or titles. Running away with her husband was the best decision she had ever made.

Chapter 4

Hugh's senses came alive as he awoke. Someone was in the room with him, and his gut told him that it wasn't The Angel. His spine stiffened and his muscles clenched, preparing for an attack that was sure to come.

Brightness from the sun shone behind his eyelids, and a gentle breeze swept across him from an opened window. The sound of noisy breathing, light and shallow, came from two persons that Hugh was certain were directly beside him.

When no attack was forthcoming, Hugh cracked an eye open and peered through his eyelashes toward the edge of his bed.

"He's awake!" a little blond-haired, brown-eyed boy whispered loudly as he peered at Hugh from his kneeling position on the floor.

"Shh!" an older, brown-haired, hazel-eyed boy admonished from beside him.

The younger boy frowned fiercely at the other. "I whispered, didn't I?"

Hugh opened his eyes fully, watching the exchange with curiosity.

The older boy turned his attention to Hugh. "My name is Quintin Bexley," he announced, puffing out his chest and kneeling higher on his knees. "I'm seven years old."

"I'm Maximus, and I'm four!" the younger boy shouted, bouncing on his knees. "Who are *you*?"

Bexley, Hugh mused. The Angel had a surname at last.

A half smile tugged at the corner of Hugh's lips. "It's a pleasure to make your acquaintance," he said roughly. "My name is Hugh."

"What's wrong with you?" Quintin asked. "You've been here for *days*."

Maximus bounced again. "Are you a *pirate*?"

"Where did Mama find you?"

"How did…"

The young lad's voice faded from Hugh's consciousness as Quintin's words registered in Hugh's mind. *Mama.* These boys were The Angel's sons. A keen—and entirely unfounded—sense of disappointment filled him. Was she married, then?

Both boys watched him expectantly, and Hugh gave them a sideways grin. "I am not a pirate."

* * *

Wiping her hands on a cloth, Charlotte turned from the hearth with a sizzling pan and scooped the cooked eggs onto four plates with a wooden spoon.

"*Four* plates, Mrs. Bexley?" Mrs. Laurie raised an eyebrow at the plates.

Charlotte's heart stalled as she remembered that Hugh's presence was to be kept secret. Mrs. Laurie aided Charlotte with the cooking and cleaning three days per week, and she was by no means loyal enough to keep something as stirring and gossip-inciting as the Widow Bexley opening her home—*and bed*—to a perfect stranger. While Charlotte cared not what people thought of *her*, she certainly cared about the impact such tongue-wagging would have on her sons. Not to mention the frightening fact that Lord Reddington was very likely aware of Hugh's imprisonment, and had either chosen to do nothing or…had taken part in it. Either way, she daren't alert him to the fact that his potential prisoner had escaped with her help. She could ill afford such dire consequences.

And, drat it, she'd entirely forgotten that Mrs. Laurie was to visit that morning. This was a visit outside of their schedule, and Charlotte hadn't remembered the addition in time.

Silence hovered in the air as Mrs. Laurie awaited Charlotte's response.

Forcing a smile, Charlotte placed the pan and hand cloth upon the worktable and turned toward the older woman. "I'd thought that you would enjoy a plate, as well, Mrs. Laurie."

The woman was petite in every way. She was short in stature and slender of build. Her angular face and deep wrinkles gave her the appearance of a severe woman, but Charlotte knew her to be very kindly, if not entirely trustworthy. The woman was an incorrigible gossip.

Mrs. Laurie's expression cleared of confusion. "While I thank you for your gracious invitation, Mrs. Bexley, I broke my fast before I arrived this morn."

Charlotte nodded sagely, relief coursing through her.

Mrs. Laurie clasped her hands together in front of her. "After I do the dusting, I will make some biscuits and feed the chickens. Is there anything else that you would like me to do?"

A squeak of alarm escaped Charlotte and she cleared her throat to cover the sound. "Er… My bedchambers do not require dusting this week. I could not sleep last night and did it myself." It was a sorry excuse, but it was the swiftest one she could think of. She hurried on. "I would be much obliged if you could instead prepare a hen so that I might cook it for the evening meal."

"Of course, Mrs. Bexley." With a curtsey, Mrs. Laurie swept from the room.

Her breath leaving her in a *whoosh*, Charlotte placed her sons' plates on the kitchen table, then prepared a tray for Hugh.

A light dusting of colour crept over her collar and up her neck at the thought of him. She'd had a shamefully lascivious dream about her house guest last night. It was entirely inappropriate, but it had been some time since she'd lain with a man, and Hugh was… Well, she'd seen him nearly entirely nude and, while his person was horribly marred by scars and he was too thin from starvation, he was still indeed sinfully attractive. His voice curled her toes, his gaze was direct but warm…and he was sleeping *in her bed*. One might consider her mad for *not* dreaming about him. Of course, one might also consider her a wanton and below anyone's notice, but that was another issue entirely.

* * *

"And where are your mama and papa now?" Hugh asked the curious and delightfully exuberant young boys.

Maximus rose from his position on the floor and joined Hugh on the bed, bouncing in his excitement. Hugh cringed at the slight jostle, but remained quiet.

The young boy leaned forward as though to impart a secret. "Mama is in the kitchens with Mrs. Laurie, and Papa is in heaven."

Hugh mentally kicked himself for his impertinence. "My condolences for your loss."

Quintin rose up to rest his elbows on the bed's edge, then lowered his chin into his palms. "I don't remember him, and Max didn't even meet him. Our papa died when Max was still in Mama's stomach."

Maximus reared back, aghast. "Did she *eat* me?"

A bark of laughter escaped Hugh before he could suppress it, and he winced at the sudden pain.

"Do you hurt?" Maximus peered curiously at him.

"Yes, I do," Hugh ground out.

Quintin frowned. "But why would someone hurt you?"

Maximus' eyes widened. "Would they hurt *me*?"

"You are perfectly safe with your mama in your home," Hugh lied. He knew nothing about the home, the neighbours, or the security. Hell, just Hugh's presence there meant danger for the whole family.

At that reminder, guilt suffused him. He hoped to have a moment alone to speak with The Angel; he must tell her to keep his presence secret, for everyone's safety. Once he was well enough recovered, he would contact his superiors and deal with Lord Reddington. But, God help him, if he sent a missive before he'd recovered and it was intercepted…there would be no chance of his—or The Angel's and her sons'—survival. Hugh could not risk their lives in such a way. Hell, even when he *was* recovered, with his clearly diminished skill at sneak-work, his chance of survival was diminished.

"You have bruises on your face," Maximus noted.

Hugh gave him a wry smile. "Indeed I do."

The boy reached out and poked Hugh's cheek. "This one is purple."

Pain spiked through Hugh's cheekbone, but he bit back the urge to groan.

"I imagine many of them are purple," Hugh replied.

Maximus wrinkled his nose. "Your face hair is fuzzy and long."

Another laugh escaped Hugh. "It is. I haven't had the opportunity to shave in quite some time."

"Did you do something bad?" Quintin asked.

Hugh's lips puckered as he considered the question. "Most everything I do, I do for the betterment of England. If someone chooses to interpret my actions as bad, then what would that make them?"

Quintin leapt to his feet, his arms held aloft. "A French spy!"

Maximus bounced from the bed to join his brother. "I shall get you, English scum!" he shouted. He lifted one arm in the air and held the other out before him, as though preparing for a mêlée. "*En garde*!"

The boys shuffled about the room, waving their arms and making clashing sounds with their mouths.

"Aha!" Maximus crowed. "I have fooled you! I brought *two* swords." He started waving around both arms.

Quintin glared at his younger brother. "I fooled you, too, for I not only have two swords, but an *entire army*! *Charge*!" He let out a battle cry and ran at his brother.

Maximus screeched and ran to the other side of the room, and despite himself, Hugh found himself being charmed.

The bedchamber door abruptly swung inward, and both boys stopped to stare at The Angel in the doorway, a tray laden in her hands and a scowl on her fine features.

"Quintin and Maximus," she said sharply. "You are not to bother Hugh during his recovery. Downstairs, the both of you; your morning meal is awaiting you in the kitchens."

The boys openly groaned as they slouched and dragged their feet toward the door.

"It was a pleasure meeting you," Hugh said, his voice gruff.

Maximus wiggled his fingers at Hugh before he closed the door behind them.

"I apologize for my sons' behaviour." The Angel placed a tray on the table at his bedside.

Hugh grinned. "Not at all. I confess I was curious to see how the battle would conclude."

The Angel returned his smile, and Hugh's chest tightened in response.

"England always wins," she assured him.

"As she ought."

The Angel kept her gaze on her task as she removed lids from the dishes. "I do hope the boys didn't pester you with questions…"

Hugh could sense the woman's curiosity. She deserved to have some answers, but Hugh was disinclined to put her in any more danger than she was presently in.

"I am not bothered by their questions. Children are inquisitive by nature."

She nodded. "They are at that." Turning her probing gaze on him, she smiled. "How do you feel this morning?"

"Much the same as last eve, but I am rested. I feel far more alert."

Her smile grew, and the vice in Hugh's chest tightened further.

"I am pleased to hear it. Would you care to break your fast? I made eggs, and there are more buns from last evening's meal."

Hugh's stomach growled, and his mouth watered at the scent of food from the uncovered dishes. "I would, thank you. Might I…" He pressed his lips together. He hated to be so dependant, but he must accept the blow to his pride if he was to eat without The Angel feeding him like a babe. "Might I have your aid in sitting up?"

Her face brightened. "Of course!"

It took several long, painful minutes, but with The Angel's help Hugh was able to sit upright in the bed, his back cushioned by a plethora of pillows. His pulse sped, and he gasped for breath as pain seized him. His injured shoulder burned, and his arm refused to respond to his mental prodding. He frowned at the dratted thing as he fought for calm.

"Perhaps a sling for your arm will keep the pressure off your shoulder?" The Angel asked softly.

Hugh nodded. "I would be much obliged."

Within minutes, she'd withdrawn a length of material from a cupboard in the corridor and tied it about his neck, resting his arm in it.

Eager to turn the attention from him—and to satiate his burning curiosity—Hugh caught The Angel's gaze and asked the question that had been tickling the back of his mind. "I hate to pry, but—"

"Quin and Max's father." The Angel pursed her lips as she nodded her understanding. She busied herself rearranging the dishes and cutlery on the tray. "Mr. Bexley died shortly after Quintin's second birthday. I was *enceinte* with Maximus."

Hugh could hear the sorrow in her voice, and the vice gripping his chest gave an extra squeeze. "I'm so sorry for your loss."

* * *

The genuine note in Hugh's voice and the sincerity in his gaze were of little comfort to Charlotte, no matter how much she wished she felt differently. The death of her husband had brought a great many truths to the fore, and none of them were… *Well.* She halted the direction of her thoughts. *They ought not be considered now.*

"Thank you," she murmured.

Hugh eyed the food with hunger in his gaze, then eagerly took a bite of egg. He groaned. "You made this?"

Ignoring the flutter to her stomach, Charlotte pulled his bedside chair closer to the bed and sat, clasping her hands together in her lap. "I did. We had a cook, a housekeeper, butler, footmen, and"—she cleared her throat of a lump that had formed there—"maids until Mr. Bexley passed. Now I employ no one. We have one woman—Mrs. Laurie—who generously offers her time, however. She comes three days per week and helps with the odd task."

He nodded, then groaned again.

Nervous fluttering rippled through her stomach once more and Charlotte silently cursed. Hugh was only human, after all. *A human with markedly alluring green eyes*, her mind whispered.

She wanted to know more about him, about his past, his personality…about who he was and what he'd been doing in a box on her neighbour's estate. Perhaps if she kept revealing information about herself, he would feel comfortable enough to confide in her, as well. Lord knew she couldn't justify interrogating a man who was so severely damaged, no matter how intense her curiosity.

Hugh took another bite of his eggs and chewed, his dark blond facial hair ruffling with the movement of his jaw.

"What of your family?" Hugh asked once he'd swallowed. "Are they able to lend their aid?"

Charlotte pursed her lips. *In for a penny…* "My family disapproved of my union with Mr. Bexley. They wished for me to wed one of my father's acquaintances, and when I expressed my regard for Mr. Bexley, they made clear their distaste for him. That night, Mr. Bexley and I eloped, and the following morning my family disowned me."

"How awful for you," Hugh said gruffly.

With a quick shake to her head, Charlotte sighed. "I have long since forgiven them for their ignorance of love. I confess, I do wish that I had seen them and my sister one last time."

Hugh's brow furrowed. "You didn't see them?"

"No. A letter from my father arrived at our inn, and I was too distraught to read it myself. Mr. Bexley read it aloud, then burned it in anger. I'd always wondered how my father had known where to find us, but in the end, it mattered not; the result would always be the same."

Without the promise of her dowry, her husband had relied on what little inheritance he had acquired from his late aunt, and the allowance from his late grandfather, in order to purchase their home and keep their staff. They lived in comfort for several years before his grandfather passed, and they were forced to parcel off some land and engage a tenant farmer.

She sighed once more, her heart heavy. "This estate was entailed to Quintin on Mr. Bexley's passing, but I will maintain it—and our one tenant farmer—until my boy comes of age."

Unprompted, her husband's most oft-repeated phrases flooded her memory. *I was trying to protect you… There are things that you don't understand… I thought this would be for the best…*

She could feel her lips tightening as she spoke, but chose instead to focus on the warmth in Hugh's gaze. "My husband proved to be rather unkind. I have never understood the purpose behind his frequent hurtful remarks or his subtle cruelty…" *Or his frequent infidelities*, she reminded herself. "But no matter how much I wished for peace, or missed having friends and family in my life, I have never regretted my decision to marry him. If I had not married Mr. Bexley, I would not have my boys, and *that* I cannot fathom."

Despite the sudden steel in his gaze, Hugh smirked. "And lively boys they are."

She huffed a laugh, grateful for the change in topic. "Indeed."

Hugh's emerald eyes crinkled in the corners as his full lips curved upward in a smile. Charlotte's heart lurched once more. *Heavens.* What about the man's smile affected her so greatly?

His dark-blond hair curled at his shoulders, tangling with the edges of his beard. What would he look like with it trimmed? What had he looked like before he'd been imprisoned? Hugh finished breaking his fast, and Charlotte mentally shook herself.

She took the tray from his lap and set it on the table. "Would you care for a book to read?"

"Perhaps later." His gaze caught hers. "I would be grateful for some more of your company, if that is not an—"

"Oh, it isn't," she assured him, cutting over his words. "Mayhap a game of cards?"

He smiled again, and her breath nigh left her body.

"I would be delighted."

"Speculation?" She rose to fetch the deck that sat in her writing desk drawer.

"I know it well enough."

She returned to his bedside, settling into her chair and smoothing out the coverlet next to his thigh before dealing their cards.

"Oh!" she breathed, the sound catching in his gut. "We've nothing with which to wager. Just a moment."

She held up one finger, then dashed back to the drawer and withdrew a small leather pouch before depositing it upon the bed.

"Buttons!" she announced triumphantly.

With a grin, he divided them in half.

"So," she said probingly, turning the top card over to reveal a seven of hearts. "I've told you about myself, but I know nothing about you, Hugh."

Hope lit in her chest as she awaited his response.

One of his bruised eyebrows quirked, and he let out a huffed laugh. "Very well, Mrs. Bexley. My surname is Stewart."

* * *

Mud squelched beneath Abraham's half boots as he led the way to their master's prisoner. Abraham and the others had been tasked with feeding and watering the blighter regularly while his lordship dealt with urgent business in town. It had been two nights since anyone had last been in to see the prisoner; their master would surely be pleased to see the progress of their torture when he returned home.

Abraham grinned to himself, anticipation bubbling just beneath his skin as he walked. The men's chatter behind him slowed to a stop as they approached the diminutive outbuilding.

"Open it," Abraham grunted to one of the other men.

One of the others hurried forward and thrust the door wide with a *bang*.

No movement came from within, and instantly, Abraham's gut sank. *Christ*, had he killed the man? He'd been tasked with keeping the prisoner *alive*! He hurried forward to peer inside. A flurry of nerves erupted in his abdomen, and dread swelled in his chest. What would his lordship do if their prisoner was dead?

"Sir!" the other man said beside him. "It's *empty*!"

Panic struck Abraham full in the chest. *Oh, hell.*

Spinning toward the other men, he knew they'd only one course of action.

"David—you, Allan, and Francis journey toward London in search of his lordship. Stop at every one of his estates and at inns along the road. He must be apprised of his prisoner's escape." Abraham set his gaze on the others. "The rest of you, come with me. We're going to search the grounds; the man cannot have travelled far in his condition."

Chapter 5

With a sigh of exhaustion, Colin Greene sat heavily upon a hidden bench in the ostentatious gardens. Aged statues, worn and marked from years of cleaning, stood in rows along the groomed grass and shrubbery, the overwhelming scent of flowers veritably choking him.

The gentle swish of fabric alerted him to the presence of his fellow, Ben, and Colin glanced his way.

"Evening," Colin said in greeting.

Ben sat on the bench beside him with a groan. "Evening. Christ, but Reddington is not even in residence, and they're working us until my body aches."

Colin's own muscles gave a commiserating throb, and he nodded. "They're afraid of him."

"With good reason." Ben stretched his legs out in front of him. "The man might be a fool ruled by his grandmother's purse, but his pride, self-importance, and unprovoked cruelty are unmatched."

"Have the servants been forthcoming? Did you learn where the bastard is hiding Hugh?"

Ben gave a quick shake of his head. "I've gleaned nothing as of yet. You?"

"The same," Colin grunted. "*Blast.* We spent too much damned time following Reddington's movements when he hadn't even left London. Would that we had thought to infiltrate his homes sooner."

"Indeed." Ben stood and cleared his throat. "He is not at this estate; we'd best move on to the next."

* * *

"Would you care to make a bid?" Charlotte inquired, lifting a brow in challenge at Hugh.

He returned her look with a quirk of his lips and a squint of one eye, his gut in turmoil. "Of course."

Shifting against the pillows at his back, he slid two buttons across the coverlet toward her.

She scoffed. "Only two? Surely you can do better."

His eyes narrowed further, and her lips quivered with mirth. Every afternoon since he had first lied about his name, they had played cards: wagering with her old collection of buttons, teasing, and discussing their interests. And every afternoon, his lie had grown larger.

He still didn't know her relationship to Reddington, or whether he could put his life—and identity—in her hands, but the larger his lie grew, the worse he felt about it. Something told him that he'd made a mistake when he'd uttered those first telling words, but there was naught that he could do about it now. Most particularly without knowing where her true loyalties lay.

With a lift of an eyebrow, Hugh added another button to his wager.

Something perverse pushed him to say, "Tell me more about your husband."

She gazed at him in thought for some time, and then spoke.

"My husband was unfaithful to me," she said baldly, her voice barely above a whisper. "I overheard people discussing it at his funeral. I was so ignorant and innocent that I hadn't even considered it a possibility. I thought we were in love. I thought *I* was in love. As it would happen, I scarcely knew the man.

"He had slept with nearly every willing married, widowed, and painted woman that he encountered. It was later confirmed by the magistrate that he'd found himself in some trouble with the husbands of his mistresses."

The words flowed from her as water rushes down a river, and Hugh could do nothing but listen. "Mr. Bexley died by drowning, was walking—intoxicated—from one mistress' home to another's." She huffed a disbelieving and self-deprecating breath. "Both women attended his funeral, in addition to three others. They wept as though they'd lost a husband, as well."

The age-old pain tightened her features as she spoke, and Hugh's heart ached for her.

"I'm so sorry for your grief, Mrs. Bexley."

"His death was the impetus to teach my boys to swim. They've swum in every lake in Leicester."

"How prudent of you," Hugh said, his chest tight with guilt.

"My husband was a skilled liar and made me feel more the fool as a result of it. I haven't trusted a man since. Until now. I've come to realize that there *are* good men in this world. Men worth saving."

Christ, what could he say to that? He'd lied to her, as well, but he couldn't sodding well tell her *now*, even if he knew where her loyalties lay.

They played in silence for several long moments before Charlotte broke the silence.

"Just more than a sennight has passed since I found you." She moistened her bottom lip with the tip of her tongue. "Has your memory returned, by chance? Do you recall what happened or who was responsible for holding you captive?"

His gaze caught hers, and his gut churned once more. If only he knew *why* she was desirous to learn the state of his memory… Could she owe Reddington in some capacity? Would she impart Hugh's response to his captor? He couldn't yet take that risk.

"I remember nothing," he lied.

The Angel's eyebrows curved upward in disappointment. "*Nothing*? Nothing at all?" She leaned forward hopefully. "What of while you were being held captive? Surely they gave you food and water, at least occasionally—did you not see someone *then*?"

Hugh shook his head in one sharp movement, hating that he was being forced to further his lies. "They were careful to never reveal their faces."

The Angel pulled her lips between her teeth, worrying the soft, pink flesh as she thought. "Did you…" She cleared her throat. "Did you happen to hear anyone speak as one would to a lord of the realm?"

Hugh's gut tightened. "I beg your pardon?"

With a nervous flutter of her eyelashes, The Angel cleared her throat once more. "Forgive me, but I must be candid. Is there any chance that my neighbour—Lord Reddington—had a hand in your capture? I found you on his land, and while I do not share an acquaintance with the man, I should like to know if my sons are in danger playing on the lands' border."

Shite. Heavy threads of guilt wrapped tightly around Hugh's insides as the truth hit him hard. Mrs. Bexley was innocent.

The lies that he'd told piled up in his mind, but as swiftly as they came, he endeavoured to banish them. There was naught that he could do about it now; he'd done what he knew to be best.

Realizing that she was waiting for his reply, he shrugged one shoulder. "I do not recall." He noted the keen disappointment in the slumping of The Angel's shoulders and the slackening of her facial features, and he knew he couldn't leave it at that. "If, however, you have any doubt of your neighbour's integrity, I would suggest that you instruct your sons to keep well enough away."

She nodded, her lips curving in a small smile. Hugh's heart gave a responding flip.

Sliding another button across the coverlet, he winked at her, attempting to return the levity to their discussion.

"Tell me of your sons, Mrs. Bexley; are they very like you as a child?"

Her smile grew and her eyes lit with joy, and Hugh knew that he'd succeeded.

* * *

Thwap. The folded newspaper hitting the inn's ale-slickened table did little to abate the tumultuous emotions in James Donohoe, the Earl of Reddington's, chest.

The war was over. Napoleon fucking Bonaparte had abdicated—the bloody bastard—leaving those loyal to him abandoned and helpless. And James was sodding helpless.

He glanced around the inn, unaccountably put out by the din of voices, the *clank* and *scrape* of the dishes and utensils, and the *thump* of mugs and tankards being returned to the tables. The threat of danger was suddenly all too…*tangible*, and far too bloody close. Surging to his feet, James wove blindly between the tables and out through the taproom's door. He gave a sharp whistle, garnering the attention of a stable hand.

A young man came trotting over, but James refused to wait. "Fetch my men and have my carriage prepared at once," he barked. "I must leave directly."

"Of course, your lordship." The man bowed deeply and darted into the inn's stables.

Left alone, James paced the innyard. There was no time left for the torture or interrogation of the bastard, Hugh Haddington. In the eyes of his curst country, James was not only guilty of kidnapping a spy in His sodding Majesty's Secret Service, but he was also guilty of torture and treason. And he couldn't have his prisoner testify against him.

His carriage rolled to a halt before him, putting a stop to his harried thoughts. Not waiting for his footman to open the door, James yanked it open and clambered inside.

"To the Lutterworth estate, urgently—we'll change horses there."

They jolted into motion, and James stared unseeingly out the window, his thoughts returning to his plight.

What he required was the wife he'd been promised and passage aboard a ship bound for the Americas. Once married, he would finally receive the stipend due to him by his grandmother, and that would provide a comfortable life once he was well enough away from bloody England.

Christ, even at this very moment, someone could be following him. Despite himself, he turned in his seat to peer out the window toward the rear of the carriage, his chest constricting with trepidation. Hell, the spies had already sent Haddington after him; it was entirely possible that they would send another… Except, now the war was over. They had no reason to merely *follow* him any longer. Now, they would attempt a capture.

With his gut twisting and his legs beginning a stuttered bounce, James attempted to set his focus as they pulled up to his Lutterworth estate. The men went about changing the horses, and James trotted inside with the intention of fetching a third set of pistols and shot. One never knew…

"Your lordship!" The butler—Christ knew his name—pulled open the front door and blinked owlishly as James strode past. "We weren't expecting you—"

"I'm not staying," James grunted as he strode to his study.

"Very good, your lordship." The man struggled to follow at his heels, but James kept his pace. "You had visitors come around—"

James halted in his tracks, turning to face the man. "What do you mean *visitors?*"

The butler's dark skin grew damp with moisture. "Y-yes, milord. Two men came a fortnight hence, and yet two more yesterday. All four inquired as to your whereabouts and wished an immediate audience."

Icy tendrils of dread clawed up his spine, and without another word, he woodenly retrieved his set of pistols and marched back to his carriage.

His world was in fucking upheaval; the bastard spies had already begun their search of him. His path, however, was clear: before he took a woman to wife and fled the country, he must return home and kill Hugh Haddington.

Chapter 6

The faint splash of water echoed softly in Hugh's borrowed bedchamber as he washed his face of shaving cream. It was the first time in the fortnight of his recovery that he had been able to leave his bed for any extended length of time without The Angel's aid. It was a great relief to have his freedom again.

Using a clean towel, he dried his skin and gazed at himself in the mirror above the wash table. Now that his facial hair was gone, one could more easily see that his skin was still slightly discoloured from his bruising and healing scars, and his knife wounds were red and puckered at the edges. He'd used some of The Angel's shears to cut his hair, which was now shorter and much more manageable, though his shoulder pained him something fierce after completing the task.

Thankfully, he'd dislocated his shoulder twice before his imprisonment, so the wound was healing rather quickly. The rest of him looked bloody dreadful.

Hugh wiped at a bit of shaving foam that had been left on his misshapen ear, then turned toward the bed, where he'd placed his borrowed attire. Mr. Bexley, though a farmer, had been very clearly a fop. His white lawn shirts had lace and frills at the cuffs, and his coats and waistcoats were covered in delicate and intricate embroidery.

With great care not to aggravate his injuries, Hugh donned a pair of fawn-coloured breeches and paired them with a brown tailcoat, a forest-green waistcoat with brown embroidery, and a white shirt, stockings, and cravat. He tugged uneasily at his too-short sleeves and watched his agitated expression in the tall mirror. The clothing was far from fitting. While he had gained enough weight to not appear sickly, he was by no means as muscular as he had been before *the incident*. Mr. Bexley's dandified attire hung from Hugh's frame, but was far too short. As ridiculous as he appeared, however, Hugh could not bring himself to complain; it was a far sight better than what he'd been wearing a fortnight prior.

A screech of laughter outside the opened window drew Hugh's attention, and he strode toward it. Below his window, Quin and Max chased each other with sticks, their laughter dancing along the air. A smile tugged at Hugh's lips, and his gaze took in the seldom-seen view from his bedchamber.

The gardens were bathed in the orange light of the setting sun, the bright rays catching on lingering rain droplets on the greenery. The gardens were veritably glittering.

Next to the grassy area in which the boys played were the gardens used for growing vegetables and fruits, and beyond that were the henhouse and smokehouse. Hugh's heart leapt when he spotted The Angel rounding the side of the smokehouse. She wore a bow and quiver over her shoulder and held two hares in her hand.

Her sons dashed over to her, undoubtedly inundating her with questions about the hunt. Hugh's smile grew.

Despite the blow to his pride and the required recovery time for his injuries, he had enjoyed the last two weeks immensely. The Angel was kind, generous, and intelligent, and her sons were amusing, inquisitive…and greatly took after their mother. His days—in between meals—were spent alternately sleeping and fantasising about The Angel.

He'd grown so accustomed to her afternoon visits that the thought of his having to move on sent a pang of regret through his chest. Their discussions had been long, but the topics of paltry significance: the weather, the land, flora, fauna, her sons, the books that they read…anything that was easily discussed without delving too deeply. So many times had he fallen asleep to the sound of her voice as she read to him that he didn't know if he wanted to sleep without her there.

The thought sent a jolt of surprise through him. It was ludicrous, of course. He was perfectly capable of sleeping on his own.

Another jolt of…something—pain?—went through him. The longer he remained, the greater the danger to The Angel and her sons. And with a knot in his gut, Hugh knew that he couldn't let anything untoward happen to them.

His brow drawn down and his jaw clenched, Hugh turned from the window and marched to the narrow writing table. He uncorked the ink and found a pen and parchment, then began to write. To the average untrained Englishman, the missive appeared to be a letter from a son to his parents, an account of his journey through the English countryside. But to a member of the Secret Service—and those spies for Bonaparte who were skilled enough to notice the code—it was a plea for immediate action.

Hugh pressed the ink blotter against the still-wet ink before he folded, sealed, and addressed the missive. For The Angel's and her sons' safety, he would send it with a courier after he'd already left the estate. As much as he wished to notify Hydra of his whereabouts immediately, Hugh daren't draw undue attention to the family that had rescued and cared for him so kindly.

Slipping the missive in his inner breast coat pocket, Hugh glanced once more at himself in the mirror. He ran a hand through his shortened hair and tugged on his ill-fitting coat before quitting the room.

He strode slowly down the dark corridor, his limp pronounced as pain spiked in his calf with each step. Tallow candles—used sparingly—sat unlit in every third sconce.

Curiosity pressed him to glance into the bedchambers as he passed them; he noted the boys' rooms, their beds haphazardly made and toys strewn carelessly across the floor. *Do they not sleep in a nursery?*

He continued on, eager to see The Angel's bedchamber.

He passed the main staircase to the other side of the modestly sized home, but the bedchambers had stopped. On that side of the staircase were a schoolroom, a sitting room, and a study and library combination. Puzzled, Hugh turned around and returned to the hall of bedchambers. He peered inside each one, but did not see another—

Awareness suddenly dawned, and Hugh's eyes widened in surprise. For the past fortnight, he had been sleeping in The Angel's bed!

* * *

James Donohoe, the Earl of Reddington, squinted into the setting sun as he disembarked from the carriage on the front drive of his Leicester estate. Gravel crunched beneath his polished Hessians as he strode to the steps, his servants bustling about around him. Absurdly, James found himself glancing into their faces in an attempt to ensure that they were his actual servants, and not spies come to capture him.

Despite the trepidation that had dogged him since he'd left that inn, he was certain that no one knew of his prisoner's whereabouts. His predicament would soon be the proverbial de-fanged tiger, once he had dealt with Haddington.

Fury had been riding him for weeks while he attended to business in London, and it was not likely to abate until his troubles were resolved. He'd received a small portion of his stipend early from his grandmother in order to give Lord Hale ten thousand quid—and his supporting vote on the man's next bill—in exchange for one of Hale's nieces' hands in marriage. But the bloody bastard had been lax in his security, and the unruly wenches had run away. Now Hale had gone and gotten himself put on trial for treason, and James had to find the woman—or an acceptable and pleasingly submissive replacement—himself.

Bloody rotten hell.

He tugged off his gloves and tossed them to one of his footmen. "Have a bath drawn and brought to my chambers, and prepare the home for closing. I intend to pay a visit to my prisoner this evening and set out first thing on the morrow."

The *clip* of his booted heels echoed in the grand foyer as he strode to the staircase at the rear.

"My lord!" his butler, Raven, called as he chased James across the foyer.

"What is it?" James snapped.

Frustration nipped at his heels. The support network of spies that he'd become a part of was slowly dwindling away. The Viscountess Evelyn was deceased, Cecil Piper had made himself scarce, Hale was on trial, Lord Bristol's whereabouts were unknown, and Sir Wycliff was already on a frigate bound for the Americas! There were but a few of them left, and with the news of the war's end, their number would undoubtedly become fewer still.

James paused halfway up the staircase as Raven caught up to him.

"My lord, we have been searching—"

"I've changed my mind, Raven," James said, cutting the man off. "I feel the need to release some tension. Have one of Mrs. Lilly's girls meet me for bed sport tonight. I'll save my bath until after I've dealt with my guest in the woods." He turned to face his butler. "Have you been keeping him alive and sufficiently tortured? At the very least, the man ought to have suffered before I dispense with him."

The blood seeped from Raven's features as he sputtered.

James clenched his jaw, irritation crawling up his spine. "For God's sake, *spit it out!*"

Raven swallowed. "We sent riders after you, your lordship, and our men have been searching the grounds for days."

Bone-searing dread burned through James, his breath all but stalling in his lungs as his man fumbled with his words.

"Searching for what, Raven?" James said, his voice scarcely above a dangerous whisper.

"Y-your guest has escaped."

* * *

Charlotte wiped her hands on a cloth before placing dishes on the kitchen's worktable. The evening's meal was a simple repast of browned partridge with gravy, buns, and cottage pie. If she'd had more time she might have thought more creatively, but as it was, she'd had to hunt that afternoon, which left very little time for anything else, most particularly after she'd had her remorseful cry.

Separating Hugh's portion out of the dishes, Charlotte plated her sons' meals then opened the rear door to the kitchens.

"Quintin!" she called. "Maximus! It is time to sup!"

"May I join you?" a low, rough voice said behind her.

Charlotte jumped and spun around. "Hugh!"

His lips curled upward in an unrepentant grin, and her heart skipped a beat in response. The man was entirely too appealing.

"Did I frighten you?" he rumbled, his gaze glittering with mirth.

Charlotte frowned at him. "You are just like Maximus to take delight in startling me so."

His smile deepened, and Charlotte had to tamp down her desire to touch his lips. He'd cut his hair and shaved his face, and though his scars and yellowed, fading bruises were more visible, he was more attractive than ever. Hugh's attire—borrowed from the deceased Mr. Bexley's trunk of clothing—was comically short, but the colours did him favour by brightening his complexion and darkening the green of his eyes.

Heat spread over her chest as she took in his tall, broad form. His appearance, warmth, and kindness were only small contributors to his attraction.

In the last fortnight, she had found herself irrevocably drawn to his company. She'd been forced to distract her mind throughout most of each day, until she could not resist visiting him any longer. And there he would be, waiting for her. They'd played cards, read, talked…and she'd relished every moment with him. It was markedly addictive.

She cleared her throat. "I see you are up and about," she noted lamely.

"I am, indeed."

"How do you feel?"

He put a hand to his injured shoulder. "I still feel the pain, but I am able to move, and for that I am grateful."

She opened her mouth to reply, but at that second her sons burst through the door and the moment passed.

"Wipe your shoes and wash your hands," she reminded them.

"Yes, Mama."

Charlotte sent Hugh a quick smile. "We would be delighted if you would join us."

His green eyes sparkled, and their corners crinkled. "I am much obliged."

The boys dashed to the washbasin and scrubbed their hands with soap while Charlotte gathered Hugh's plate and put it on the table across from hers, her stomach all but entirely in knots. Giving herself an internal shake and determinedly ignoring the feelings the man inspired in her, she added both coffee and tea pots to the table.

"Mama!" Maximus sat hard on his chair beside her. "Guess what I found this morning!"

"What did you find?" She smiled down at him as she took her seat.

"A toad!" he announced triumphantly.

Charlotte wrinkled her nose. "Did you, indeed?"

"And *I* found a snake," Quintin added. "I didn't touch it, though."

"I should hope not."

"Did you find snakes and toads when you were a young boy, Hugh?" Quintin looked up at Hugh, who gingerly lowered to the seat beside him.

Hugh nodded thoughtfully as he took a fork to his piece of cottage pie. "Most definitely. My younger brother and I would spend hours—"

"You have a brother?" Maximus interrupted.

Hugh stilled, his eyes going carefully blank. But then he blinked, and the perplexing expression was gone.

"Not a brother, but a very good friend." He took a bite of his pie.

"What's 'e like?" Quin asked around a mouthful of partridge.

Charlotte put her fork down. "Do swallow your food before you speak, Quin. And Max, remove your elbows from the table, if you please. We are not beasts, for pity's sake."

"Yes, Mama," the boys mumbled in unison.

Hugh looked at her questioningly as he pointed to the pots on the table. "Is this…?"

"My apologies." She dabbed at her lips with a napkin then gestured to the pot in front of him. "That one there is coffee, and the other is tea. I rather enjoy them during the evening meal. If you would prefer, I could fetch some—"

"This is perfect. Thank you." His eyes squinted in a pleasing sort of smile as he poured himself a cup of coffee and added a generous spoonful of sugar. "My friend is two years my junior," he said to the boys, "and he is a very talented goldsmith in London."

Charlotte listened intently as Hugh spoke, curious to know more. While she had avoided any direct questions about Hugh's past—and had secretly hoped that he would offer information without her having to ask—they *had* discussed events from their childhood. And to her surprise, twin blades of pain and disappointment lanced through her.

She swallowed a suddenly flavourless bite of her partridge, then poured herself a cup of tea. "He must be worried about you."

Hugh nodded. "Indeed, he must."

Charlotte spooned sugar into her tea and began to stir, the gentle *clink-clink-clink* of the spoon against the porcelain filling the room. The hairs on the back of her neck stood on end, and she glanced up, catching Hugh's amused look. Her gaze lowered to the spoon in her teacup, and she pursed her lips.

"Judge me for being uncouth if you wish, Hugh," she said defiantly, "but I do not care for the sugar settling at the bottom."

A grin lit his face and the breath rushed from her lungs, her previous ill feelings vanishing like dust in a breeze. How she wished she could see him smile thusly forever.

Betraying nary a bit of the surge of desire rushing through her—she hoped—Charlotte arched a brow as she added cream to her tea and stirred it in, as well.

Hugh barked a laugh, and suddenly Charlotte feared she might become sick. Because surely no one could endure the riot of fluttering in their stomach and not embarrass themselves.

"Your face isn't hairy anymore, Mr. Hugh," Maximus noted.

"You are correct, Max; I shaved this evening."

Hugh's gaze caught hers across the table, intense and, if she were not mistaken, *heated.* Her mirth faded, and a deep, burgeoning desire quickly replaced it. She wanted to embrace the feeling, to give in to the need to feel a man's lips on hers, his hands on her body…but the sensible part of her mind whispered that men could not be trusted.

If she did not wish for a courtship or marriage, however, could she not simply enjoy a man's touch? Surely she was not the only woman who required the comforting intimacy that such an arrangement could provide. She *was* a widow, after all…

With a hasty redirection of her thoughts, she instead listened to her sons regale Hugh with stories about their imaginary battles. They were currently describing a difficult bout with a great horned beast that they claimed lived in the rose bushes in their gardens. Next, they conjured up inquiries about what would happen if a bee were to grow to the size of a horse and a horse shrank to the size of a bee.

"The bee's stinger would be easy to avoid, because it's so big!" Maximus shouted, his arms stretched wide above his head.

Quintin rolled his eyes. "But it would be *so* big that it would definitely hit you!"

A deep pout curled Max's lip, and he turned to Hugh. "What do you think, Mr. Hugh?"

He gave them a half smile. "Truth be told, I would be more concerned with how to make carriages travel. Would we strap the giant bees to them, do you suppose? Would we fly everywhere?"

The boys' eyes widened in unison, and they stared at each other with glee.

"As truly diverting as this conversation is," Charlotte began, "it is time for bed."

Quin and Max groaned loudly, and Charlotte *tsked,* rising from her seat. With a tightening of his jaw, Hugh stood. She wanted to urge him to remain seated and rest, but she appreciated the demonstration for her sons.

"Come along, boys. We must brush your teeth and read your evening story."

She turned to leave, her sons scuffing their feet on the flagstone floor as they followed. But before she was through the door, Charlotte glanced over her shoulder at Hugh, and heat rushed through her once more. "I shan't be long."

Chapter 7

Utter terror twisted every corpuscle in James' body as he crouched next to the chains that had restrained the filthy English spy, Haddington, and examined the locks. He held a handkerchief to his nose and mouth—the stench of the little outbuilding nearly unbearable—as he turned the shackle over with his other hand.

The edge of the manacle's keyhole was freshly abraded, the metal scraped from the picking of the lock. He dropped the manacle back to the water-dampened floor with a muffled *thud* and looked about. The bastard had escaped. But *how*? And where would he go? Would he return directly to London and into the protection of his little spies, or would he play on the sympathies of one of James' tenant farmers, or one of the neighbours in the surrounding estates?

Fuck. The man held power against James, and he couldn't allow that to stand. Haddington *must* be found. And he had to die.

With an imperceptible nod, James rose from his crouch and slowly made his way out of doors to search around the building.

"We examined the area, your lordship," Raven said as he approached. "We weren't able to find anything."

"Cretin," James uttered gutturally. "The evidence is here; one must merely know where to look. Unfortunately, enough time has passed that learning the direction our guest and his accomplice took is nearly impossible. This is your bloody fault, letting this happen!"

"I'm ever so sorry, your lordship." Raven shuffled his feet. "Perhaps we had best—"

James cut him a scathing glance. "I said *nearly* impossible, Raven. I will not give up now. I *will* find Haddington, and when I do, I'll be sure to remain at his side to ensure his long and painful demise."

* * *

Decorum be damned, Hugh rested against the back of his chair, his legs outstretched beneath the table and his stomach pleasantly full. Throughout the entirety of the evening meal, The Angel had stolen glances at him from beneath her eyelashes, and, every time, Hugh's heart squeezed in response.

The glances she'd sent him left him feeling light-headed, and more than a little heated beneath his cravat. Before his abduction, Hugh would have already seduced the woman, healing wounds notwithstanding…but with *her*, something stopped him. He'd never before taken the time to build a rapport with a woman, never cared whether or not she spoke to him after he'd had his fill of her. But with The Angel, Hugh found—*alarmingly*—that he cared very much.

As he trailed his gaze along the path she'd taken with her delightful sons, a strange sensation washed over him. He was suddenly full of restless energy and a desire to—*no*. That way lay madness, surely.

Rising to his feet, Hugh picked up several dishes, strode toward the washbasin, and deposited them on the work surface to the side. He gathered more and placed them beside the washbasin, as well, his healing body protesting each movement. Truthfully, he found the pain encouraging, and a sign that he ought to continue to move.

"Oh!" The Angel gasped, coming to his side, and Hugh was overcome by her clean, earthy fragrance. "Your aid is much appreciated, Hugh, but do not overtax yourself on my behalf."

"My pain is minimal," he lied. "I would very much like to help you."

She smiled again, and Hugh's speeding pulse belied his calm exterior.

"I thank you, then." She gestured toward the pot above the fire. "If you would, please fetch me that kettle."

Hugh did as The Angel bade while she lathered soap against a rag in the bottom of the large washbasin. The kitchen was grand for a home so modest in size, but Hugh suspected that it had been specifically designed for Mrs. Bexley's use. She moved about the kitchen with a grace and comfort born from years of use. The hearth was enormous for a country home's kitchens. Curious, though, that Mrs. Bexley hadn't opted for a new closed range; apparently they were all the rage in the well-appointed homes in London. While she mightn't be a wealthy Londoner, it was obvious that The Angel spent a great deal of time in that room and could likely use the convenience of a closed range.

Hugh poured the hot water into the washbasin of cool water, the steam rising up to stick to the hairs on the back of his hand and create a damp film on his face.

"Thank you," The Angel breathed, her soft voice hitched with what sounded like…

Hugh's gut tightened, and he glanced at her quizzically, but she'd already turned to scrape the uneaten food from the plates into a separate bin. With an internal shake, he returned the kettle to its hook over the hearth and gingerly removed his coat. Rolling up his too-short shirtsleeves to bare his forearms, Hugh set to washing the dishes. He was a man accustomed to various living conditions, and knew well how to do his own cleaning.

After scraping the plates, The Angel fell in beside him with a cloth for drying. They worked together, him washing the dishes and her drying them and returning them to their proper place.

The air between them was silent and dense, the room filled with the lingering scent of their evening meal and the overwhelming fragrance of soap. Hugh wanted to believe that the tension between them was only their undeniably raw attraction, but somewhere in the back of his mind he knew it was largely due to his withheld truths…and his lies.

The truth would endanger The Angel and her sons, putting them in even greater peril than they were already in just by having him in their home.

As much as he detested the unhappy reality of his circumstance, Hugh knew what must next be done. He would stay on for another day, perhaps two, but then he would take his leave of The Angel and her sons.

The thought sent a schism of unease through him and made his sodding chest ache. *Bloody hell.* It would seem that he had unconsciously been forming an attachment to his rescuer and her wonderfully mischievous sons.

"Are you well, Hugh?"

He blinked, his pulse speeding and his gut twisting, then returned The Angel's gaze. "Of course," he lied, forcing a smile. "Why do you ask?"

She gestured to his soap-lathered hands, mirth tugging at her lips. "You have been scrubbing that last plate as though it has done you a disservice. Have my dishes offended you?"

"My apologies," he muttered, dipping the plate into the adjoining washbasin to rinse it in the clean water. "I had not realized…"

The Angel placed a hand upon his forearm, and Hugh's muscles tightened.

"Is there something bothering you?" she asked.

A great many things. "Not at all, I assure you." He withdrew his arm to dry his hands upon another cloth.

Her lips thinned and her brows knit as she considered his reply, her disbelief written plainly on her fair features. It was another thing he adored about her. She was not coy; she did not toy with his emotions like a practised lady of the *ton*. His Angel wore her emotions on her proverbial sleeve.

She removed her thin white apron to reveal a serviceable pale-green frock and tossed the apron haphazardly upon the worktable. Her light-blue eyes assessed him, some unnameable emotion shuttered in their depths. "Would you care for a game of cards?" Her voice was soft, breathy.

Hugh nodded, his throat abruptly dry.

The Angel turned to leave, but Hugh touched the sleeve of her dress to stop her. She watched him quizzically, but in that moment Hugh did not know what to say. He'd wanted to convey his gratitude for all that she had done: for saving him, for housing, clothing, and feeding him…for keeping him company and giving him her bed. But his words would not come.

Instinct drove him forward as he slowly closed the distance between them. The Angel's eyes warmed, her face flushing a delicate pink that accentuated the dusting of freckles along the bridge of her nose and high along her cheeks.

Hugh's heart raced as he thought of giving in to temptation and kissing her. What would she taste like? The thought caught hold of him with preternatural strength, and his gaze dropped to her full, rosy mouth. Internal warning bells notwithstanding, he cupped her jaw, drawing his thumb across her bottom lip.

A stuttered gasp escaped her, and his body thrummed with the need to taste her. She blinked slowly, the desire he saw there reflecting his own. But he wouldn't presume…

"I must confess," he began, his voice husky, "I have thought of kissing you for some time."

The Angel's throat convulsed as she swallowed. "Have you?" she whispered.

"Yes," he breathed, watching her grey-blue eyes closely. "Would you permit me to kiss you, Mrs. Bexley?"

* * *

Charlotte's stomach swirled and swooped with nervous anticipation and her heart fluttered as Hugh caressed her lips with the pad of his thumb once more. Another ripple of desire coursed through her abdomen, her gaze flicking upward into his striking green eyes.

Despite her earlier qualms about giving in to desire, she did not need to consider her answer. "Yes."

He moved achingly slow, closing the space between them with care and caution. The lingering scents of spices from their evening meal and the dish washing soap in the washbasin hung in the air, but all Charlotte could smell was *him*. He smelled of shaving soap and coffee.

Her breath came quickly as he dipped his head toward her, his gaze intent on her lips. Charlotte put one hand to Hugh's waist and gripped his bared forearm with the other. His skin was warm, his soft hairs damp from the water.

Charlotte tilted her chin upward as Hugh slid his hand to the base of her neck, his fingers catching in her hair and his thumb tracing along her jaw. She couldn't remember ever being touched in such a way by a man. To her amazement, a soft groan escaped her lips, and her head swam with desire, leaving her feeling decidedly unsteady before he'd even kissed her.

Hugh wrapped his other arm about her waist, pulling her against his front. Charlotte's heart skipped. He might have grown thin from malnourishment, but he was lean and muscular after weeks of regaining his strength.

An impatient whimper escaped her as he prolonged the moment, letting the air between them veritably crackle. Need swelled inside her before he finally captured her lips with his. Her skin sizzled at the contact, and her grip on him tightened as her jaw slackened. She wanted to feel more, *taste* more.

Tensing his arm around her waist, Hugh teased her tongue with his, gently flicking and lapping. And she matched him with equal fervour, her chest heaving with each breath as an explosion of raw want burst from within her.

Warmth spread over her skin and through her abdomen, the molten desire pooling in her core. Oh, yes, she wanted more.

So many years had passed since Charlotte had been kissed that she'd forgotten how very wonderful it could feel. After her first year of marriage—and the birth of Quintin—Mr. Bexley had stopped kissing her altogether. But never had it ever been like *this*. The luxurious, languid building of nascent need that made her want to climb his body in blind lust.

His mouth, soft and heady, moved over Charlotte's, then suddenly he pulled away. Keen disappointment lanced through her. It was too soon; they'd scarcely begun! Her pulse thrummed, and she could hardly catch her breath…

Hugh caressed her cheek, a sad smile on his features as he gazed at her. "Thank you, Mrs. Bexley."

Charlotte resisted the cringe that threatened at the sound of her married name. "Please, call me Charlotte."

Something flashed behind his eyes as he nodded. "You saved my life, and for that I will be forever in your debt."

His words held a note of finality that settled heavily on her chest. Realization dawned on her that he intended to take his leave soon.

They stood thusly for several heartbeats as discontent swept through her. She did not want to miss this opportunity to *feel* again.

Without giving herself a moment to consider her actions, Charlotte carefully encircled Hugh's shoulders and neck with her arms, rose up on her toes, and kissed him.

Chapter 8

Charlotte's heart soared at Hugh's immediate response. His previous kiss, while sensuous and arousing, only heightened her desire without satisfying it. This one would be different.

She ran her hands over the breadth of Hugh's back, committing the feel of him to memory. His shoulders were angular, the blades on his back jutting out as he wrapped his arms tightly about her waist. His muscles moved beneath her palms, bunching and stretching over his ribs.

His lips were soft, and tasted of coffee and shaving soap, the tart yet sweet flavour rousing her senses. Charlotte inhaled deeply of his scent, logging it in her mind, as well. She wanted to remember everything about that moment so that she might replay it in her mind on long, lonely nights.

A gasp escaped her as Hugh slid his hands from the small of her back to the fullness of her bottom…and squeezed. Charlotte instinctively arched into him, pressing her body against his. Hugh responded in kind, making her keenly aware of the hard ridge of his erection that pressed insistently into the soft flesh above her *mons*. Tingles of awareness shot down her spine, and heat gathered once more in her core.

As though somehow ignited by a spark, their kisses turned frantic. Her desire took control of her body as she clung to him. A low groan rumbled from Hugh's chest. Their breath mingled as their tongues danced erotically.

Charlotte wanted more. She wanted to have Hugh's hands on her skin, to have his mouth on her breasts, to experience the basest human intimacy of contact. Lord help her, she wanted to make love to the man.

Hugh broke their kiss to slide his lips along the side of her flushed neck. Charlotte moaned, raking her fingers through his hair to urge him on.

Her patience all but entirely gone, she reached for the buttons of his waistcoat.

"Charlotte," he growled. "Are you sure—"

"Yes," she cried.

With a guttural groan, Hugh lifted her and spun them around until he'd deposited her on the edge of the worktable. She released his shoulders and brazenly lifted her skirts over her knees, exposing the entirety of her legs, stockings, and garters to his view. His hands immediately found the tender skin of her upper thighs as he slotted his hips between them.

The hard ridge of his erection nudged her dampened cleft, and she sighed, needing far more than the light touch could give her. Her hands went to his falls, trembling slightly as she unfastened his buttons and urged his cock free. She was at an ill angle to get a glimpse of him, but she cared not. She needed him *inside* her. *Now.* It had been five years since she'd lain with a man, and her body didn't want to take it slow.

Without a second's hesitation, she dipped her own fingers into her heat, swirling and gathering slickness before she spread it around the engorged head of his erection.

"*Holy Christ*, Charlotte," he breathed hoarsely. "That was—"

He leaned forward to capture her mouth in a ravenous kiss. Gripping his hips, she urged him forward, and he guided himself inside with one hand.

His lips pulled back on a hiss as his intense, steely heat filled her.

"*Oh…* Oh, Hugh, that's— My God, you're so—" She raked her fingers up his back and in his hair, wishing that she could touch his skin.

He cupped her arse and slid unhurriedly out, the movement agonizing in its slowness.

"Fast," she urged. "Please, Hugh, I need it fast."

"Happy," he grunted, thrusting with each word, "to oblige."

Pleasure rocked through her, and she dropped her head back as his hips moved, his cock deep inside her. His lips found her neck, and he pressed open kisses along the column.

Heat suffused her body, and her limbs began to tremble. "*Oh, Hugh,*" she cried.

Her paroxysm was building, but, unable to wait, she reached between them and pressed her fingertips to her cleft.

Hugh pulled back to watch, his eyes wide and his hips still thrusting. "*Fuck*, Charlotte, are you—?" A guttural moan rumbled through his chest, his face flushing.

Chasing the pleasure, she flicked, twirled, and rubbed until a tingling rush swept up from her toes and crashed through her, throbbing and utterly glorious. Her body shook, and her head fell back on a keening shout of completion.

Hugh gasped and cursed, then withdrew from her sheath to spend on her kitchens' floor.

"*Charlotte*!" Hugh growled, his teeth bared in a grimace and his hands squeezing her bottom as tremors shook him in his own pleasure.

They remained thusly for several long moments, their breath coming rapidly. As her passions cooled, Charlotte became very aware of her exposed legs, and with a flick of her wrists, she drew the material down.

Hugh cleared his throat and stepped away, tucking himself back into his breeches, and giving Charlotte the space to drop down. The silence stretched as they righted themselves, and Hugh cleaned his seed from the floor with his cravat.

Nerves swam in her abdomen, and all at once, she decided that it oughtn't be that way. What was wrong with taking her pleasure when it suited her?

"I needed that," she said baldly, turning a shy smile on Hugh. "Thank you."

A quick smile flashed over his features, and he swept in for a buss to her lips. "Thank you, as well."

* * *

His shoulder aching fiercely, Hugh ran trembling fingers through his hair as he closed the door to his borrowed bedchamber the next morning. His swift bootfalls were muffled on the carpet runner, his pulse and feet speeding with anticipation.

Charlotte, his mind whispered. The Angel's name was Charlotte. It suited her.

He'd thought of nothing but her since he'd departed the kitchens the previous evening, his dreams filled with feverish touches and passionate kisses that had him stiff and aching upon awakening.

Other women rarely inspired anything in him but the basest of desires and the human need to satisfy them. But Charlotte made him *burn*. His heart, his gut, and even his *mind* were engaged in a way that was entirely foreign to him.

Sodding hell, but their tryst had been…entirely unexpected. In more ways than one, to be sure. Not only had he *felt* things with which he was not familiar, but, *Christ*, Charlotte's utter avidity, even now, had the power to tighten his cods.

With an internal rebuke and a discreet shift of his trousers, Hugh strode into the kitchens.

Plumes of flour filled the air and dusted every surface, while Charlotte stood at the worktable punching a large ball of dough, a smear of flour marring her forehead.

A smile tugged at Hugh's lips. "Good morning."

She brushed aside a lock of fallen hair with the back of a knuckle, leaving another powdery stripe along her temple. It was painfully endearing.

"The morning meal is cooking," she said, gesturing to the hearth behind her. "This is a loaf of bread that will be ready for tea this afternoon."

"Would you care for some help?"

Her eyes widened in surprise before she blinked. "N-no, that's quite all right. I wouldn't wish to aggravate your injuries." A pretty pink stained her cheeks.

The loud *thunk* of the door knocker echoed through the house, eliciting a groan of frustration from Charlotte. "I must answer that," she said breathlessly as she wiped her hands on her apron and attempted to fix her hair. "Please await me here; no one knows of your presence…"

Hugh nodded. "Of course."

The door knocker thudded once more, and with one last glance toward Hugh, she dashed from the room. Another increasingly impatient knock sounded at the front door before he heard Charlotte open it.

"Good morning to you, Mrs. Bexley." Lord Reddington's smooth, supercilious drawl echoed through the foyer.

Hugh flinched at the sound of his captor's voice, his heart racing and his healing wounds throbbing as though with memory.

"Good morning, Lord Reddington," Charlotte returned. "Won't you come in?"

There was a slight hesitation before Reddington replied, "I should think not."

Swift relief rushed through Hugh. He understood Charlotte's conciliatory gesture, but it would be unlucky if Reddington entered.

Lord Reddington continued, "I am come to inquire about a guest of mine that has gone missing. He was thrown from his horse on a hunt several weeks past, and injured his head. I'm afraid he has become quite confused and seems to have wandered off."

Hugh tilted his ear toward the foyer as he struggled to hear the remainder of Reddington's words.

"…light brown—almost blond—hair, green eyes, tall, and thin."

"My sincere condolences for your friend's injury." There was a faint humming sound before Charlotte continued. "I have not seen anyone matching that description in town, nor on my lands. I will, however, be sure to inform you immediately if I do; I wish you the very best of luck."

"And your sons?" Reddington pressed, his voice ominously low. "Might we ask *them*?"

"My sons are focusing on their studies at the moment, your lordship, but I am certain that they would alert me to a stranger's presence immediately if they saw one."

Hugh's stomach knotted tighter. Reddington was suspicious.

"Should we search the home, milord?" another voice asked, most likely that of a servant.

Hugh's breath caught in his throat as silence filled the air, everything hanging on Reddington's reply. In his mind's eye, Hugh could picture the beastly man's face as he considered his answer, his green eyes—not unlike Hugh's own—narrowed in thought, his lips twisted and puckered simultaneously.

"No," Reddington drawled.

The breath Hugh was holding left his lungs in a *whoosh*.

"Mrs. Bexley would be foolhardy to be dishonest with us…after all, a life hangs in the balance."

The remainder of the interchange faded from Hugh's consciousness as Reddington's thinly veiled threat rang in his ears.

The bastard would clearly do anything to have Hugh in his clutches once more.

Hugh had no choice in his next course of action: in order to protect his rescuer and her delightfully mischievous sons, Hugh must reveal his truth, and leave immediately.

It was evident that his secrecy did nothing to protect Charlotte and her sons from Reddington's notice, and her further ignorance would only serve to prevent her preparedness for her potential fate. The Angel might very well decide to abscond to Scotland, or return to the bosom of her family, in order to flee Reddington's machinations. Or, as Hugh would advise her, she could tell Reddington a skewed version of the truth and hope that he is lenient.

Whatever decision she came to, the woman deserved Hugh's honesty.

The *thud* of the front door closing echoed in the foyer, and the weight of what was to come loomed darkly over his soul.

* * *

The oak door's cool surface did little to soothe the heat in Charlotte's palms. She leaned forward to place her forehead between her hands, the soft *thunk* scarcely audible over the racing of her heart and the muttering of Lord Reddington and his men as they shuffled down her front steps toward their carriage.

Holy hell! Hugh had lied to her, the scurrilous bastard. And she'd engaged in a *tryst* with the man, for Christ's sake!

An anguished groan escaped her, the sound bouncing off the door and sounding loud to her ears.

Her body trembled with fear, hurt, and rage, the three emotions warring for control. The telltale prickle of tears threatened behind her eyelids, and the sharp sting only furthered her fury. Fury at Hugh…and at herself.

How could she have been so undiscerning?

Squeezing her eyes shut against the painful ache in her heart, she pushed away from the door and took a deep, trembling breath, the scent of tallow wax and wildflowers momentarily filling her senses before she exhaled. The *clip-clop* of horses' hooves and the *crunch* of gravel under carriage wheels faded down her front drive, and she turned and strode determinedly toward the kitchens.

She pressed the latch and swung the door inward to see Hugh sitting at the table, seemingly at his ease, his legs stretched out before him, his elbows resting on the chair's arms. But his eyes told her that he knew what was coming; he'd heard Reddington's inquiry and was awaiting her return. He stood slowly, his shoulders taut.

Her stomach fluttered at the sight of him, and her anger flared. The lying cad did not merit such reactions in her body.

She frowned fiercely and hid her trembling fingers in the folds of her skirts. "I must insist, Mr. Stewart, that we have a proper and *honest* discussion." Her voice quavered, and she cursed the flurry of anger and nerves rushing through her.

His gaze never left hers, but his full lips thinned into a grim line as he nodded, gesturing to the table with one hand. "Shall we be seated?"

No, her heart screamed. She wanted to remain standing, to maintain a stance of control… But the threatening wobble in her knees left her without a choice.

Her spine stiff and her fists carefully clenched, Charlotte rounded the table and sat. Hugh took the chair across from hers, his mien resolute.

"Who are you?" she asked baldly.

"I'm Hugh—"

"*To Lord Reddington*," she clarified.

In what appeared to be an unconscious gesture, Hugh rubbed a hand over his healing shoulder. "I am his enemy."

Charlotte squinted. "How so?"

He closed his eyes on a heavy sigh before he pinned his piercing green gaze on her. "My true name is Hugh Haddington. I am—"

"You gave me a *false* name?" she asked incredulously.

"I did." He inclined his head. "I am a crown spy in His Majesty's Secret Service, and Lord Reddington is a traitor."

Resisting the urge to roll her eyes at yet another very obvious falsehood, Charlotte ground her teeth.

"I am," Hugh continued, "what we in our band of spies calls a 'tail.' I follow suspected traitors and report their activities, whereabouts, and possible cohorts back to my superiors in the Home Office. I was assigned Lord Reddington as my target, and I followed him for several days. Clearly my ability to go undetected has slipped, for Reddington laid a trap for me and brought me to his estate to be tortured for infor—"

Charlotte scoffed, breaking off Hugh's long-winded lie. He blinked, visibly confused by her reaction.

She leaned forward, resting her elbows on the table, her anger abruptly bubbling to the surface. "Do you genuinely expect me to believe this fantastical lie?" She paused briefly, but continued before he could reply. "How *dare* you tell me falsehoods when my sons' lives could very well be at stake? I took you into my home—into my *body*—and nursed you back to health, and you repay me by engaging in this ridiculous charade?"

"There are things that you don't understand, Charlotte. I thought it was for the best that I hide the truth, for your protection and that of your sons."

The heat of fury rose to her cheeks as her husband's oft-used platitude and excuse slipped from Hugh's lips. Hell, but she'd *bedded* the man—another liar just like her husband!

"You dare to—" Her words cut off as he reached out to clasp her hands, but she swiftly wrenched them away, cupping her palms against her abdomen.

Hugh sighed. "I am not lying to you, Charlotte. If Reddington should question you further, it is imperative that you know the truth. You could tell him that you'd seen me, but I'd stolen a horse and rode off toward town, or that I'd appeared in your home and threatened you, demanding food and your silence. You could tell him that I was holding a gun to you when you'd answered the door, and you were too afraid to tell him that I was there, for fear of your life. I would advise that you then tell him the truth of my direction; it would be your only saving grace if he threatens you."

A quick frown creased Charlotte's brow as her disbelief fumbled with the possibility that he might be speaking the truth. *He's a liar*, her mind whispered. *He betrayed me*, her heart cried.

Perhaps he'd gotten into debt with gambling, cheated at cards, or he'd slept with Reddington's mistress, but the fact that Hugh had so little respect for her that he would spin such obvious tales hurt more than she cared to admit.

The terrible fact remained, however, that Reddington could use Hugh against Charlotte and her boys. The man was powerful and had influence in the *haute ton*, and while she was not raising her sons in *society*, she did wish for Quin and Max to make a good life for themselves. Reddington could take that from them.

If there was a way to mitigate the enmity between the two men, though, perhaps she could remove the risk of danger to her sons…

"Please, Hugh," she urged. "I wish for you to feel confident in your ability to confide in me. Whatever trouble you are in with Lord Reddington, I'm certain that there is a way out of it."

Hugh pinched the bridge of his nose before he raked his fingers through his dark-blond locks. "I *am* confiding in you, Charlotte. Lord Reddington is a very dangerous man…" His voice faded as he caught Charlotte's narrowed gaze.

She had further questions for the man, but if he intended to lie to her, what would be the point of asking them?

"I confess, Mr. Haddington, that I'm rather disappointed. I'd hoped that we might engage in an open discussion, particularly after—" She stopped herself short of embarrassment. Her lip began to tremble, and she caught the rebellious thing between her teeth.

The truth of the matter was, she was hurt. Deeply. It was her own dashed fault, of course, for letting him affect her so thoroughly. She'd been so blinded by his charm and his wit—much like she had with her husband—that she'd been unable to face the truth of his deceitful character.

"I believe it would be best if I left." He rose from his seat.

Strangely, his retreat hurt her more. Her stomach twisted alarmingly and her heart grew heavier.

Despite the miserable feeling, she stood with determination, her spine stiff. He was correct, of course. "Indeed it would."

"Might you have a mount I could borrow?"

She nodded, sighing in resignation. "My husband's gelding, Percy, is in the stables. He's not been ridden in some time, but he's been exercised and he loves people. And I cannot in good conscience allow you to leave without taking some coin. I store an emergency stash in the tea tin in the larder." The man might be a liar, but he still deserved to live, for pity's sake.

"You have my thanks." Hugh straightened his coat sleeves as he pinned her with his emerald stare. "I vow I will repay you with interest. I will stay at The Seven Stars in town. Should Reddington return, you ought to give him my direction. If you have need of me after the morrow, I will make a stop in Brampton before returning to Lon—"

The heavy *thud* of the front door's knocker echoed through the foyer, putting a halt to their moment in the kitchens for the second time that morning.

Alarm spread through Charlotte's chest. Had Lord Reddington returned so quickly? Would he demand to search her home?

"Go on with you, now," she whispered as she urged Hugh toward the kitchens' rear door. "I will answer the door. You take Percy and ride into town."

Obviously sensing the urgency of the situation, Hugh reluctantly did as he was told and strode toward the door. With his hand on the latch he turned to look at Charlotte over his shoulder. "If you should require me after I've returned to London, head to White's—"

"But that's a gentleman's establishment!" Charlotte interjected.

He inclined his head. "Knock on the rear door, accessible by the alley. When someone comes to the door, request a meeting with Rupert Grimly. You will be shown into a private meeting room, and a letter will be sent to my fellows and me. Help will be there directly."

Another knock sounded at the door, and Charlotte waved her hands at Hugh. "Very well. Now, shoo! Off with you!"

He dashed out the door, and the thought briefly entered Charlotte's mind that he wasn't attired properly for a ride, nor did he don a hat, but she brushed it aside. There were more urgent matters at hand.

Chapter 9

Charlotte pressed the front door's latch and swung it inward just as the knocker fell, thudding against the wood. Outside stood two tall, sombre-looking men wearing serviceable suits of clothes.

"Good morning, madam," one man said, holding his tall hat to his chest. "My name is Colin Greene, and this is my friend Mr. Brown. We have come in search of our friend—"

With a short shake to her head and irritation overruling her decorum, Charlotte cut over them. "You are not the first men today to come looking for their injured friend," she said. "Do you share an acquaintance with Lord Reddington?"

The silent man's jaw clenched as Mr. Greene cleared his throat. "No, we are not."

"And are you also in search of Mr. Hugh Haddington?" she asked.

Mr. Greene's lips thinned, and Mr. Brown finally spoke. "Yes. We last saw him in London, but we learned that he'd travelled to Leicester several months ago. We are asking masters of the local estates if they have seen or heard anything about him."

Despite the fact that Hugh had urged her to tell the truth about his presence at her home and his intended destination, he had scarcely been given enough time to reach the stables, let alone saddle and mount a horse. He needed more time to escape! She might be angry with the man, but she by no means wished for his death.

Charlotte's heart was still aching from her interaction with the dratted man, and the misters Greene and Brown's prevaricating was too much to be borne. She did not for one moment believe the tale these men span. "I'm afraid that I must disappoint you gentlemen, for I have not seen or heard from anyone matching your friend's description. Perhaps another local farmer will have better news, though I would recommend your asking Lord Reddington first, for he seemed to know much more than I. Best of luck in finding your friend. Good day."

She dipped a short curtsey as she unceremoniously closed the door.

* * *

Colin Greene raked his fingers through his thick, dark hair as worry knotted his stomach. Hugh and Gabriel Ashley were Colin's best friends, and it hurt them greatly when Hugh had gone missing all those weeks ago. After the attacks on their fellow Secret Service spies, Colin had feared the worst.

They'd been in suspense since Gabriel had recently learned of Hugh's location. Gabe had been on assignment, and had heard the scurrilous bastard, Reddington himself, admit to keeping Hugh captive on his Leicester estate. Naturally, Colin and his fellows had hastened to search for him. They'd found a stinking, fetid box in the woods with irons fastened to the floor to keep him there—but no Hugh.

"The woman was lying," Brown muttered as they strode toward their mounts.

Colin nodded, relief flooding him. "Indeed. I imagine he was here for a time, but I do not believe him to still be in residence. Hugh would not have caused undue risk to an innocent woman."

Knowing that Hugh was alive, however, gave Colin some semblance of comfort. And hope.

Leather creaked and their geldings huffed as they mounted.

"Curious that she would lie about seeing him," Brown mused.

"Yes, curious."

Colin suspected that Brown was alluding to a possible romantic entanglement, but Colin knew it to be impossible. Hugh was popular with women, to be sure, but he was not the sort to keep a woman once he'd had her.

They nudged their mounts toward the road, the *crunch* of hooves on gravel filling the air as Colin ruminated. The sun shone down between white fluffy clouds, warming him through his brown coat, the feeling at odds with the icy dread growing in his stomach.

"Mrs. Bexley's mention of Lord Reddington concerns me," Colin confessed. "The man's uselessness and self-infatuation are at odds with how very dangerous he is. If the bastard is in pursuit, then we have little time in which to find Hugh. Now that the war is over, Reddington will be desperate to be rid of any ties to Bonaparte and any question of his loyalties."

Brown inclined his head. "If Reddington gets to Hugh before we do…" He left the thought unfinished, though Colin knew the point he was making.

Colin's gut gave another anxious squeeze. If they didn't reach him, Hugh would die.

* * *

"Mama, Mama!" Quintin and Maximus shouted in unison as they entered the kitchens.

Charlotte swallowed her mouthful of chilled tea before she placed the cup back on its saucer, the ache in her heart and the anger in her gut weighing heavily on her. "Yes, boys?"

"We've finished a *lot* of work," Quintin said, emphasizing his words by spreading his arms aloft.

"Yes, *a lot*," Maximus repeated.

Charlotte bit back a smile as she shifted her seat on the chair by the table. "Have you completed your work with maths?"

"Well…" Quin shrugged one shoulder. "Maybe not all of it, but we did—"

"A *lot*!" Max lowered his voice for dramatic effect as he cut over Quin.

"And we want to go outside!" Quin jumped up and down.

Charlotte cut them a sharp look. "Now, now," she scolded. "How do we ask politely?"

"May we please go outside?" they asked, though slightly out of sync.

"Yes, go on with you."

The boys cheered and dashed away, eliciting a light laugh from Charlotte as she cleared her tea from the table. She would join them to continue their lessons that afternoon, but for now they would benefit from some time out of doors.

Hugh had not re-entered from the stables, so Charlotte assumed that he'd ridden away. The throbbing ache that had settled into her heart returned at the thought of him. She knew that there was no sense in thinking about him. It was likely that she would never see the man again, and she ought to be pleased with that fact—he'd deceived her, after all. But the ache would not abate.

She placed the cup and saucer in the tepid, murky sink water, paused, and brought her fingers to her lips…remembering.

With a shake of her head, Charlotte turned, resolving to not think of him for the remainder of the day. She straightened her apron and set to work.

Over the past weeks, she'd used far more tallow candles than she'd budgeted for, so she would have to prepare some rushes for rush lights and melt the nubs of old candles in order to use every available bit of wax. With that in mind, Charlotte went to the larder, where she'd stored the freshly plucked rushes, then brought them to a large pot that sat filled with water near the hearth. She placed the rushes in the water, put a lid on the pot, and then hung it over the low-burning fire.

Humming a tune in her head—and decidedly *not* thinking about Hugh—she strode about the home, gathered every candle end that she could find, and brought them back to the kitchens, using her apron as a sort of net. She set aside a strainer—with which she would filter out the wicks and any debris lodged in the tallow wax—and retrieved a tin of congealed mutton fat for the rush lights.

With that project prepared, Charlotte gathered boxes of peat and set them beside the main hearths about the house, then did the same with the small amount of coal that she had last budgeted for. She then returned to the kitchens and checked on the boiling rushes. They weren't quite ready, so she stoked the fire and gathered the ingredients for crumpets.

A light tapping sounded at the rear door to the kitchens and, surprised, Charlotte called entrance, knowing whom it would be.

"Good morning, Mrs. Bexley," Mrs. Laurie called as she strode through the doorway. "You hadn't yet sent word on when you wished for me to return, but I made a rather large stew and thought that I would bring it over."

"Oh! My goodness, Mrs. Laurie, thank you! How very thoughtful." Charlotte greeted her with a kiss to the cheek. "Your timing, in fact, is fortuitous, for I've need of you today."

"Excellent! Where are we starting?" Mrs. Laurie removed her gloves and adjusted her mobcap before retrieving her apron from a peg on the wall and donning it.

Gesturing toward the hearth and worktable, Charlotte filled the woman in.

"You've had a busy morning, Mrs. Bexley," the woman noted. "I will continue with the tasks here in the kitchens, shall I?"

With a sigh, Charlotte patted her half-fallen hair. "Thank you, Mrs. Laurie. I will tend to the bedchambers; the bedclothes require changing."

She gave the woman a half smile before she quit the room and traipsed upstairs. It would be pleasing to sleep in her own bed again. But first, she must rid it of *Hugh*.

She strode through the door, and halted. The bedclothes were rumpled, and a discarded pair of stockings and smallclothes lay on the floor. Hugh's enticing scent of soap, coffee, bergamot, and…*him* penetrated the air, and a deep, sudden longing weighed in her chest.

He lied, she reminded herself, disappointed that she was so affected by his leaving. *He's a cad, just like your husband was.*

Her gaze scanned the bed, and the chair that had been placed to one side of it. She'd sat in the chair, playing cards and reading books to Hugh, for a fortnight. They'd discussed many topics, laughed…

Charlotte pressed her lips together in a line as her heart gave a decidedly heavy *thump*.

With an internal shake, she stiffened her spine and strode forward, straightening furniture and gathering linens to be laundered. She opened the window to rid the room of his scent and allow the fresh, warm breeze to filter in. Clearing the wash table of Hugh's shaving implements, she emptied the washbasin and returned the items to a box for storage.

She removed the pillow coverings, determined to exchange them for ones that Hugh hadn't used. The last thing she needed was to smell him all night. Lord knew what kind of dreams she would have…

Her stomach twisted and fluttered simultaneously, and she scowled. Charlotte's foolish emotions would not bring Hugh back, and she wasn't even certain that she wished it. He'd lied to her, and then he'd abandoned her before rectifying his falsehood. She ought to be pleased that he was gone. Indeed, she would forget him soon enough.

Chapter 10

Maximus shifted to sit on his knees, the fresh scent of hay tickling his nose. He dug in his pocket for some pilfered meat from Mama's smokehouse before a warm nose poked at his hands, and ticklish whiskers brushed his fingers. Max giggled.

"May I feed him a piece?" Quin asked, his hand outstretched toward Max.

With a nod, Max tore a chunk of the meat and handed it to his older brother. Mama's horse shuffled in the next stall, bumping against the thick wooden wall that separated them.

Orange moved to sniff at Quin's hand, his tiny paws lifted. Quin ripped a small piece of the meat and let Orange take it.

"I think Orange has grown a lot, don't you, Quin?" Max asked as he stroked the kitten's soft fur.

Quin sighed. "I've told you, Max, Orange is a silly name for a cat."

"But he likes it!"

"I think we should call him Duke." Quin fed the kitten another piece of meat.

Max looked sideways at the kitten as he stuffed the remainder of the meat in one pocket and pulled a shallow dish from his coat's other pocket. "What about Eugene?"

Quin made a face. "No."

Max tapped his chin with his finger, looking around their favourite stall. Piles of hay lined the small space, and some of their tin soldiers stood in battle positions on top. Max took a deep breath, smelling the hay, leather, and horses.

"Aha!" he exclaimed. "What do you think of Milton? Or *Frederick*!" he shouted.

Mama's horse whinnied.

"I don't like those, either." Quintin wiped his palms on his trousers before withdrawing the small bottle of cream that he'd stored in his coat. He removed the lid and poured some into the dish that Max had brought.

"I have the perfect name!" Quin smiled at Max, his dark, mixed-colour eyes alight with triumph. "*Jack!*"

Maximus eyed the tiny orange kitten, his fur striped and wiry, his grey-blue eyes cast downward as he lapped at his dish of cream. He still rather liked the name Orange, but Jack suited the kitten well.

"I like Jack," Max said, giving the kitten another pet and a scratch behind the ear.

Little Jack looked up at them, a drip of cream dangling from his chin, and Max laughed. "Silly Jack."

Quin pulled a bit of hay from one of the piles and dragged it along the hay-covered floor of the stall, garnering Jack's attention. Quintin wiggled the strand, and Jack pounced.

Laughter bubbled up from within Max. "I want to try, too!" He pulled some hay from one of the haystacks and dragged it along the floor.

Something made a *thump* near the door of the barn, and Quintin put a hand to Max's arm, halting his movement.

"Shh." Quin put a finger to his lips.

Oh no. Mama didn't like it when they played in the stables. She said it scared the horses. They would be in trouble and have to do more work if she caught them!

"Stay here," Quintin whispered.

Max nodded, sitting silently while his brother stood and stepped out of the stall.

He heard a gasp, and some shuffling feet, but no one spoke. Something didn't feel right. Quin would have said something. *Mama* would have said something. Maybe it wasn't Mama.

Scooping up Jack, Max stuffed the kitten in his waistcoat against his chest.

There was another shuffle of feet, and Max's heart turned over. Something out there was wrong. He rose slowly to his feet and crept toward the stall's entrance, peeking his head around the corner.

Three men stood in the middle of the aisle—one was tall and dressed fancy, while the other two wore servants' clothing. The two servants held Quin, one with his hand over Quin's mouth. The gentleman muttered something under his breath and waved a pistol in the air.

Max's heart all but stopped as the air got sucked from his lungs. He wanted Mama. The gentleman spun around, his angry green eyes piercing like daggers at Max's stomach.

With everything he could muster, Max took a deep breath and let out an ear-piercing scream.

* * *

Charlotte gave one last tug to the counterpane on her bed, straightening out some wrinkles, before she moved to take the pile of unclean bedclothes out of the room. She was bending to retrieve them when Maximus' sharp screech floated in through the window.

Heaving a sigh, Charlotte strode to the window and bent outward, craning her neck in order to get a view of her land and the edge of the stables. "Be kind to one another, boys," she called.

She listened carefully for their customary reply of "Yes, Mama," but when it wasn't forthcoming, she called again.

"Please refrain from fighting, boys!" she called louder.

Still, there was no response. Could Maximus have been hurt? Concern rippled through her, and she quickly strode from the room. The hallways seemed to narrow on her as she dashed through them. Making her way down the stairs and out the rear door, she broke into a run toward the stables. She knew the boys liked to play in there, despite her wishes. Had they spooked her mare? Could Max have been trampled?

Horrid images flashed through her mind of her boys' potential injuries, causing her heart to flip-flop and her stomach to knot. She rounded the side of the house to find the stable doors open.

"Quintin?" she called. "Maximus?"

She ran inside, down the aisle, halting before their favourite stall. Tin soldiers stood proudly atop the hay, a dish of cream sat nearly finished, and the bottle lay toppled upon its side. A pang of fear sliced its way through her heart.

Spinning on her heel, Charlotte ran from the stables. "*Quintin*!" she screamed. "*Maximus*!"

The rumble of horses' hooves and carriage wheels on the gravel of her front drive chilled her to her soul. *No!* She sprinted around the house just as Mrs. Laurie came careening through the front door.

"*Blackguards*! *Cads*!" Mrs. Laurie screeched as she dashed onto the drive. She turned, spotting Charlotte running toward the departing carriage. "The children, Mrs. Bexley! Those men have Max and Quin!"

Charlotte's frantic gaze caught on the Reddington family crest emblazoned on the side of the carriage, and her blood ran cold. She knew of what that monster was capable.

"The men forced the boys into the carriage," Mrs. Laurie continued.

"Mrs. Laurie, could you—"

"Go, child! Go! I will take care of the house."

"Thank you." Charlotte nodded, then broke into a run toward the stables.

Skipping the tack room, Charlotte dashed directly to her mare's stall; there was no time to saddle Leela. She would have to ride bareback.

"There, there, Leela," she said soothingly as she patted the horse's shoulder. "We need to go for a ride. Are you ready, girl?"

Without waiting for a response, Charlotte slid the stool over, lifted her skirts to her thighs, and climbed awkwardly onto Leela's back. She fisted one hand into the mare's mane, wrapped her other arm around Leela's neck, and urged the horse into a gallop.

* * *

His stomach in knots, Hugh took a swig of ale before returning the tankard to the table's surface, feeling decidedly too ill to eat luncheon. He stared into the tankard, his thoughts still engrossed with Charlotte.

Was it Reddington who had returned to question her? Surely Hugh would have heard her shout if something untoward had happened.

Lord, but he was a coward! Not only had he hurt her feelings, but he'd also abandoned her to face potential trouble on her own. No matter how hard he tried, he couldn't expel her hurt expression from his mind's eye. He felt like a scoundrel, both for hurting her *and* for leaving her.

He ought to have told her sooner; he'd had plenty of time to discuss his life while they'd played cards and ate their meals together, but he'd always prevaricated. Hugh could only imagine how much his lies must have hurt her, particularly after they'd shared such intimacies.

If he'd told Charlotte the truth of his life earlier, would she still have wished to kiss him? His gut told him that she would, but then, his gut had been recently discovered to be unreliable.

Hugh ran the scenario through his mind, practising the words he ought to have said. He thought of holding her tighter during their kisses, as he'd wanted to do. He remembered lifting her onto the worktop, positioning himself between her thighs, and kissing her neck. His thoughts ran rampant with lust, recalling their tryst…and then he imagined assimilating himself into her life while also maintaining his duties in the Secret Service, of helping her raise her sons in a house in London, of making love to Charlotte every night for the rest of his life, being able to taste her sweet skin and run his fingers through her brown hair as she rode him into oblivion…

"Is there summat wrong wi' th' ale, then?" A taproom maid appeared beside him, and Hugh jumped.

He cleared his throat. "No. The ale is fine."

The girl nodded and turned to the patrons at the next table. Hugh glanced around and shifted in his seat, hopeful that no one would notice the sorry state of his trousers. It was, perhaps, not the best of times to be ruminating on such things.

He hastily took another gulp of his ale—paid for with Charlotte's meagre funds—and put the tankard down, refocusing his thoughts—decidedly *away* from intimacies with Charlotte.

While on his ride into town, he'd considered his options for attempting to make things right with her.

Hydra and his fellows would have been searching for him. As soon as he'd claimed a room at the inn, he'd copied his coded missive and sent both out: one to the school in Brampton—Grimsbury Manor—and one to Hydra in London. He knew not what state his band of spies was in, or if anyone was able to help, but he hoped that by tomorrow evening there would be reinforcements there to help him—and hopefully aid with the payment of his tab. At the very least, his fellows would know that he was alive.

It would be at least four-and-twenty hours before one letter reached Grimsbury Manor, for the posting boy would wish to change horses, rest, and sleep along the journey, but the letter to London would take less than half the time. He was certain, however, that there would be fewer men able to help from London, as they would all be occupied with assignments.

Hugh would remain in Leicester while he awaited aid. No matter how much he wished to return to Charlotte in order to draw Reddington away from her, he must remain distant…at least until he had help. If he were fully healed, he would not hesitate to fight Reddington on his own, but even he must admit that he would not survive such an encounter, no matter his training.

There was uproarious laughter across the room, and Hugh watched the men at their table. One man clapped the other on the back while another pounded his fist upon the table in amusement. At another table, a man sat quietly reading a newspaper, and at another, a couple ate a meal and conversed quietly. In front of them sat two matrons in mobcaps talking animatedly on one topic or another.

The space was of good size for an inn's taproom, though uniquely ornamented for the room's purpose. It was rectangular, with the bar on the far left side and the main entry on the far right. At least a dozen tables filled the space in between. To the front of the building was a row of windows looking out toward the innyard, brightly lit by the midday sun, and to the rear of the room were a blackened, cold fireplace set deep into the wall, and a stairwell leading to the abovestairs rooms. The upper half of the walls was painted a light blue, and the bottom half was white-painted panelled wood. The decorations gave one the impression of a sitting room or a parlour, not a taproom that served spirits.

He caught one of the matrons staring at him, and he nodded. Hugh knew how he appeared, with his ill-fitting attire and fading bruises and scars from his brutal imprisonment; it was merely an inconvenience that he now drew so much attention to himself.

How much did Hydra and his fellows know about his capture? Had they figured out that it was Reddington who had taken him? Or that it was Charlotte Bexley who had rescued him?

Returning the tankard to his lips, Hugh swallowed the last of his ale. The morrow could not come soon enough. He needed to make things right with Charlotte.

Chapter 11

"*Blast*!" Charlotte barked, causing Leela to waver beneath her. "We lost the confounded trail."

She stroked the mare's neck as she scanned the road ahead of them, then turned to look behind them. The carriage containing her sons and the bastard, Reddington, must have turned down a side road. They had ridden well past the Reddington estate, so she knew that they hadn't gone there.

Where is he taking my boys?

Her pulse raced and her breath came quickly, sweat tickling a path down her back and between her breasts as she stared anxiously down the road. Damn, but she couldn't catch her breath, couldn't move, couldn't breathe, couldn't think!

Pain radiated through her quavering thighs and up her back and shoulders. Riding bareback was unfamiliar, and it strained muscles that she didn't often use.

"What do I do, Leela?" The panic in her voice was palpable.

The familiar sting of tears prickled behind her eyelids, but she forced it away. She would not give up hope. She *would* find her sons.

But how?

Charlotte worried her bottom lip between her teeth. Her skin felt too tight for her body, her tumultuous emotions veritably bursting for release.

She growled. "We cannot stand here all day, Leela! What do I do? *What do I do*?" The question replayed over and over in her mind, circling so fast it nigh made her dazed.

Reporting the abduction to the magistrate would likely prove fruitless. He had no motivation to believe Charlotte—a widow who had been disowned by her family—over a lord of the realm.

What was it that Hugh had said about Lord Reddington? *Lord Reddington is a traitor... He is a very dangerous man...* Her heart hiccoughed, and she placed a hand over her chest as both fear and hurt rushed through her.

I vow I will repay you with interest. I will stay at The Seven Stars in town… Hugh's voice rushed through her mind, and she knew at once what she must do. The man might have hurt her feelings, but he was her only hope to save her sons.

"Come, Leela," she said with determination, and turned the mare around. "We need help."

Urging the horse into a gallop, Charlotte pushed past her discomfort, eager to reach her destination. Lord knew what she would face on her journey, but it would behoove her to go armed. Indeed, she would ride home to retrieve her bow and quiver. Then she would go to town and plead for Hugh's aid.

* * *

Hugh dabbed his lips with a napkin and placed it beside his empty plate. If he hadn't become so hungry for luncheon, he'd not have eaten the fare. The beef was tolerable, if bland, but everything else was barely palatable and coated in a slimy substance that Hugh couldn't identify. It was a meal that would sustain him, however, which was precisely what he'd required.

Placing one arm upon the table, Hugh took a draught of his second tankard of ale while he surreptitiously slid the serrated beef knife into the inner breast pocket of his coat. He might have had to vacate The Angel's home quickly, but he'd be damned if he went without a weapon. Reddington was still in search of him, and Lord knew when they might cross paths. If he weren't still recovering from his injuries, Hugh would be able to fight without the use of weaponry, but such was the circumstance.

An older gentleman at the table next to him grumbled and folded the newspaper he'd just opened, then turned to Hugh. "This one's old. Would you care for it?" He held the paper out to Hugh.

Hugh nodded. "I thank you, yes." It had been some time since he'd been abreast of the goings-on in London.

Smiling, he accepted the paper and pushed his plate away from him so that he could open it.

On the front page were the big, bold words: *The War Is Over: Napoleon Bonaparte Abdicates.* Hugh's heart stopped, then began to pound. He eagerly opened the paper, flipping to the first—and largest—article. He read the first few lines, and his jaw dropped.

A taproom maid came by and took his plate, but he'd scarcely noticed as he read the words that proved the horrid war had ended. He read and reread the words several times before it finally sank in.

The war was over. The article read that they'd taken great losses on both sides at the Battle of Waterloo on June 18, 1815, but France's was substantially greater. It goes on to say that shortly thereafter, on June 22, Napoleon Bonaparte abdicated for the second time.

Unbidden, tears fell over Hugh's lashes to streak down his cheeks, relief flowing through his veins. His chest heaved; he felt nigh ready to burst. His body buzzed with energy; the need to run, jump, or shout tightened his skin.

The entry door abruptly swung open, the force of it banging against the outside wall and drawing Hugh's blurred gaze. Standing in the doorway was a harried-looking Charlotte, a bow and quiver slung across her back and her gaze scanning the room. Hugh put the newspaper down, wiped at his cheeks, and stood. She spotted him, her shoulders slumping as she sighed.

Desire and sheer relief at the news of the war's end drove him toward her. He strode purposefully forward, determined to make things right with her. Walking to within arm's reach, Hugh extended his arms toward her, prepared to bring her into his embrace.

But then he noticed it. The tear trembling on the edge of her eyelashes, threatening to fall. *Something is wrong,* his mind whispered. All at once, the elation that had spread through him fled, his blood running cold. *Something terrible happened.*

Instead of embracing her, his hands stopped on her shoulders in concern.

"What is it?" he asked in an undertone. "What's happened?"

"It's the boys." Her voice wavered. "Reddington's taken them."

Hugh's heart all but stopped in his chest. *It cannot be!*

"What of the gardens? Perhaps they've just meandered farther from home than usual?" he asked hopefully.

Charlotte shook her head, her lip quivering. "I heard Maximus scream… I saw Reddington's carriage."

Terror lanced through Hugh's chest. Reddington was not a particularly intelligent man, but he was ruthless, maniacal, violent, and petulant, which made him one of the most dangerous men that Hugh had ever encountered.

He gazed into Charlotte's blue, watering eyes and gave her shoulders a light squeeze. "We *will* retrieve them," he assured her.

Spinning, Hugh located the innkeeper several feet away, and called over to him. "My good man! Have my mount saddled, if you please."

The innkeeper nodded. "Right away, sir."

Hugh turned back to Charlotte and clasped her hand in his. "Come."

Striding quickly through the taproom and up the stairs, he led her to his bedchamber, where he locked the door behind them and marched to the writing desk. Gratefully, his writing implements were still out from earlier. He sat at the desk, sliding a piece of parchment toward himself and dipping the pen in the ink.

"What was their direction?" he asked Charlotte, who stood anxiously near the door.

"North." Charlotte shook her head. "I could only speculate as to his intended destination. Perhaps Nottingham or Leeds…"

Hugh nodded as he began writing the coded letter. With a few scratched sentences, he replaced the pen to the inkpot and waved the parchment through the air to dry the ink.

"To whom are you writing?" Charlotte asked from her position by the door.

Folding the parchment, Hugh wrote the hasty direction on the back. "This morning I wrote to my superior and my fellows, both in Brampton and in London, informing them of my situation and requesting their aid in taking Reddington down. If they arrive while I am gone, I wish for them to know my direction."

Not waiting for Charlotte's reply, he lit a candle on the low-burning coals in the hearth and returned to his seat to melt seal wax over the folded parchment.

"Have you a mount?" he asked.

The Angel worried the leather strap that crossed her person, which held her quiver in place. "I do. Though I daresay she's exhausted from the ride here."

Hugh strode toward her, the letter clutched in his hand. "The few minutes' respite will have to suffice. The grooms will have watered and fed her by now."

He put a hand to her elbow, and his body instantly reawakened with desire, the heat seeping deep into his aching heart. Now, however, was most certainly not the moment for such feelings, so Hugh tamped down on his body's urge to pull her into his arms, and instead led her down the corridor and back to the taproom. Even had it been the appropriate time and place for a passionate embrace, Hugh couldn't countenance any delay knowing that Quin's and Max's lives were in peril. Every second counted. Additionally, he hadn't yet reconciled with Charlotte, and he sure as hell didn't want to feel as though he were taking advantage of her fragile state.

They strode to the innkeeper, and Hugh handed him the letter. "In roughly four-and-twenty hours, someone—possibly a group or a pairing of people—will come here looking for me," he told the barrel-chested man. "They might merely offer you my description, or they may ask for me by name—Hugh Haddington."

The innkeeper nodded. "Arright, then."

"When they do"—Hugh tapped the letter that the innkeeper held between forefinger and thumb—"give them this letter."

"Very good, sir." The innkeeper jutted his jaw toward the taproom's entry. "Your mount is saddled and ready in the innyard."

"Thank you." Hugh withdrew several coins from his pocket and handed them to the big man, whose eyes grew wide at the sum.

Hugh turned to Charlotte. "Are you ready?"

The Angel bit her lip, but nodded.

* * *

Charlotte pulled on Leela's reins, slowing her to a walk, both of them out of breath and bone-weary from the long ride. Hugh drew up beside her, his mount slick with sweat and huffing each breath. Charlotte glanced up at the darkening sky, and her stomach twisted painfully.

When would they find Quin and Max? How did they fare? Lord, but they must be so frightened!

She took a deep breath, schooling her features and suppressing her tumultuous emotions. "Perhaps we are on the wrong road," she hedged. "It has been some time since we've seen a sign of anyone's using this one."

"It is difficult to tell in this light." Hugh combed his fingers through his wind-blown dark-blond hair. "Our horses require respite. We ought to stop at the next inn. While we are there, the horses will be watered and fed, and you and I can question the innkeeper and have a meal."

Charlotte hated to stop, but she knew that they had no other option. Their mounts could not run further, and neither could she deny the hunger pangs gnawing at her stomach. "Very well."

The *clip-clop* of their horses' hooves was muffled on the packed dirt road. The surrounding farmlands, shrubbery, trees, and long estate drives grew even more obscure as the sky gradually darkened. Clouds swept in high above them, blocking out the light from the stars and moon.

A chilled gust of wind blew swiftly past as Charlotte slid a sideways glance at Hugh. Her stomach flipped over, and she cursed her body's lack of qualms when it came to including Hugh in her search for her sons. The man continued to withhold the truth from her, as well as lie outright. It was a wonder she'd asked for his aid at all when the hurt he'd caused her was still achingly fresh. But the pain of losing her sons was greater. Whether she was pleased about it or not, she needed Hugh.

Trusting men had, at one time, been commonplace for her. But since Mr. Bexley…

"I wonder at Reddington's location," Hugh mused, pulling Charlotte from her dark thoughts. "Does he wish to draw me out, or did he desire a word with *you* on ground where he was in control? In either circumstance, he would not have driven far."

He combed his fingers through his hair as he thought, his chin jutted and his lips pursed.

Truthfully, the question of what Reddington wanted sent shivers up and down Charlotte's spine. "Mayhap he is cross with me for having helped you escape," she suggested.

Hugh shook his head in a dismissive gesture. "What matters now is retrieving your sons."

That was certainly true.

They entered a curve in the road where the surrounding trees grew dense, and Charlotte saw it. Farther around the curve, through the branches, were lights from windows.

"An inn!" She notched her chin toward it.

Eager to get their respite over with and be on their way again, she urged Leela faster.

Chapter 12

Hugh attempted a polite smile as the barmaid placed food on the table. Internally, however, his stomach roiled and his heart was pinched with worry. He very much feared that Reddington was toying with him as a means of *emotional* torture. It would undoubtedly be a way of punishing Hugh for escaping, and it was certainly something that Reddington would do merely for the enjoyment of it.

He wondered at Reddington's motivation. The man's behaviour did not quite make sense. Was he luring Charlotte or Hugh? He must have known that further torture of Hugh would not yield any results. One thing was certain, however: at its crux, this was not about Charlotte and her sons; this was about Hugh. Reddington must be desperate to garner control of the man who could see him hanged for treason, and he was using two innocent boys and their mother as a means for manipulation. The bastard.

"Is there anathin' else I can get fer ye?" the young, freckled barmaid asked as she eyed Hugh with open curiosity.

His smile grew brittle. "I thank you, no. This will do well."

The lass strode away, and Hugh frowned. He was aware that his appearance might be startling, but the stares that he'd received since arriving had become unnerving.

"Where do you think Reddington has taken my boys?" Charlotte whispered as she poked at her braised pigeon with the prongs of her fork.

Hugh's gaze travelled over Charlotte's downturned features, a pang of compassion jolting through him. "Reddington is a coward. He will find a place in which he believes he will have full control. Possibly an abandoned building, somewhere with small, enclosed rooms."

Charlotte mulled over that information. "If he wishes for you to find him, would he not find a place that is secluded but easily accessible?"

Hugh swallowed a mouthful of bland potato and considered the question. "Not if he wishes to play with me, to make me work to find him. The longer he eludes us, the more he knows we will suffer."

"Hugh, do you…" She swallowed, the colour leeching from her cheeks. "Do you think that my sons will be—"

She pressed her lips together, unable to give voice to her fears.

Hugh put his fork down and reached across the table to clasp her hand in his, giving his silent support. "I followed Reddington for some time. I became familiar with his habits and his way of conducting business. He was never respected among his traitorous peers—his intelligence and gift for planning never quite matching the others—but he comprehends consequence. I'm certain that he understands that if the boys are harmed, he will not attain what he desires."

* * *

Charlotte wanted to ask further questions, to learn more about why Reddington had so abused Hugh—Hugh's lies were not answer enough for her—but at the moment all she could think about were her sons, and what horrors they were facing. Did they cry out for her? Were they hurt? Cold?

The stiff hold that she'd had on her control abruptly broke. Her chest heaved on a silent sob, and her chin quivered, tears welling in her eyes as her whole body trembled with heartache.

"*Christ*," Hugh cursed. He slid his chair around the table, stopping as its corner bumped against hers, then he sidled close, their thighs touching.

Another sob shook Charlotte's frame. Her skin tingled as grief crashed through her in waves.

"Come here." Hugh opened his arms to her, and she gratefully accepted his embrace.

Tears flowed freely from beneath Charlotte's lashes, her sorrow aching deep in her soul. Her heart stung, and her lungs felt as though they wouldn't take in air. The brief hopefulness that she'd felt earlier crumbled further with every minute that passed.

With slow strokes, Hugh ran his palm in circles over her back. "Shh, shh," he hushed. "We will find them."

She pressed her forehead to his neck, nuzzling into the soft spot between his shoulder and jaw. The short growth of beard high on his neck gently abraded her skin and further mussed her hair, and he carefully gathered the strands and tucked them behind her ear.

Her shoulders trembled with sorrow beneath Hugh's arm, and he tightened his hold. She breathed deeply of his subtle bergamot scent, the familiarity and the warmth of his touch bringing a small sense of comfort.

Charlotte's tears seeped from between her closed eyelids, flowing over the bridge of her nose and onto Hugh's coat. Despite her determination to remain strong for her boys, Charlotte forgave herself this moment of weakness. A maniacal madman had captured her beautiful sons and taken them Lord knew where in order to draw out another of his torture victims. The right to a moment of grief was most certainly hers to take.

Hugh's warmth seeped into her bones, and her hysteria began to calm. His sturdy strength and unruffled confidence bolstered her fortitude. He cupped the crown of her head and pressed a firm kiss to her brow. In another circumstance, Charlotte might find the gesture forward but, at the moment, she rather needed the silent gesture of support.

* * *

The *snick* of the bolt sliding into place echoed in the small, dimly lit room, and Maximus Bexley's heart pounded with doom. His bottom hurt from the bad men pushing him to the hard wood-planked floor, but he resisted rubbing it, hovering one hand protectively over the squirming mass in his waistcoat.

Quintin's hand tightened in his, their palms sliding against each other with their collective sweat.

"Are they gone?" Max whispered, swallowing past the lump in his throat.

Quin nodded. "I think so."

The squirming in his waistcoat intensified, and Max let go of Quin's hand to release Jack. The orange kitten tumbled awkwardly to the floor, then watched Max with an accusatory glare.

"I'm sorry, Jack." Max smoothed out the kitten's fur with his palm. "I couldn't let the bad men know that we had you with us."

Quin stood and strode about the room while Max watched him. There was an old wooden desk pushed into one corner, and a broken chair piled on top of it. Beside the desk was a rolled-up rug and a tattered chaise longue on its side. The rest of the room was empty but for long, thick, scary cobwebs and the pieces of peeled green wallpaper that had fallen to the floor.

Dim light from a window lit the room, and Max pointed to it. "Can we escape out the window?" He stood and followed his brother toward it, Jack bumbling along behind him.

Quin pushed on the window's glass and tested the edges. "It doesn't open," he said. "If we break it, the men will probably hear."

He turned to Max, his fear written plainly on his face. Max's stomach turned over, and his chin quivered, tears springing to his eyes.

"Do you think Mama is mad at us for playing in the stables?" he asked, his voice weak. "She warned us not to... She said that something bad might happen."

Quin shook his head, his eyes swimming, too. "I don't think that she meant something like *this*."

They were silent for a few moments before Max's stomach growled. He covered the sound with one hand, and then he remembered. "I have some smokehouse meat left." He reached in his pocket, withdrew the big piece, and broke off a chunk, handing it to Quin.

Quin popped it in his mouth and chewed as Max broke off another smaller chunk and bent to give it to Jack before he took a bite for himself.

They each had another bite, and then the pilfered meat was gone.

Max pressed his back to the wall and slid to the floor, bringing his knees up to his chin. Jack pounced onto his shoulders and nestled against Max's neck. A sad smile stole over Max's lips as the kitten began to purr.

"Will Mama ever find us, do you think?" Max asked, his voice muffled against his trousers.

Quin sat down close beside him. "I don't know, Maximus."

Something in Max's chest burned as fear and sorrow heightened in him. He'd been scared when the bad men took them, and during their journey, but now that they'd stopped, all he could think about was Mama. He missed her.

"I want to go home." Tears splashed Max's knees as they fell.

Quintin sniffled. "Me too."

* * *

Sir Charles Bradley sat, eating luncheon at the writing desk in his temporary bedchamber at Grimsbury Manor, the spy school in Brampton. He'd arrived but a few days prior to both continue the searches for Hugh and Richards and to visit with the recovering Christian Samuels, their lead cryptologist.

In the short time that Charles had been at the school, he'd seen the evidence of Samuels' deep love for his new wife, furious though she was with him. Charles' lips tugged upward in a grin.

A throat cleared in the doorway, and Charles halted with his fork halfway to his mouth to look up at the school's acting butler.

"My apologies, Hydra, but an urgent letter has arrived for you." The young man bowed.

"Thank you. Bring it here." Charles gestured the man forward.

He accepted the letter from the silver salver and read the direction.

"My God," he breathed. "It cannot be."

He tore the letter open and read, his gaze scanning the coded document several times before he slammed it down on the table next to his abandoned cutlery.

"Alert the stables!" He dashed from the room, halting in the foyer where he knew his voice would carry. "*Roundup*! Hugh is alive and needs our help!"

* * *

A few drops of rain were brought on a cool breeze, hitting Hugh along his forehead and cheeks. The sky had long since grown dark, and despite the hours of riding, they had yet to find any sign of Quintin and Maximus.

Charlotte slowed her mount to a walk, and Hugh pulled on Percy's reins to match her speed.

She turned her defeated gaze on Hugh as she curled a lock of fallen hair behind her ear. The motion caught his eye, and he had to tamp down the desire to lean over in his saddle and reach across the space between them to twirl the coffee-brown lock around his finger. In fact, he wanted to do a hell of a lot more. Though his focus was on their search, Hugh continued to wonder if there was a chance that he could not only make things right with Charlotte but also renew the affection that they'd once shared.

"We must be nearing the midnight hour, and a rain has started," she noted, her voice heavy with loss. "I worry that we mightn't find them tonight."

Hugh's stomach tightened with apprehension, and the feeling caught him by surprise. His level of attachment to this assignment concerned him.

His jaw clenched as he considered the facts before them. They'd been riding; therefore, the distance to their quarry should be gradually closing, as the carriage travelled at a slower speed. There was a very real possibility that Reddington wished for Hugh to catch up with him and, if that were so, finding where they'd bedded down for the night ought to be simple, even in their current blanket of darkness. He must keep in mind how the bastard himself would view his place of hiding—where would he go? What would he do?

"We will push on," he told The Angel. "And we *will* find them tonight."

They rode on, the mounts gradually slowing with exhaustion and their coats growing slick with sweat and the lightly falling rain.

Charlotte's jaw jutted at a thoughtful angle in the muted moonlight. Hugh wished the clouds would clear so he might see her face in the full light of the moon, her skin bright in its milky glow.

"Look!" Charlotte exclaimed, her index finger aimed at two distinct carriage tracks leading off of the main road.

Shame washed over him, tightening his gut. He ought to have kept alert. Christ, but his skills were well and truly slipping. The reminder tightened the knot of horror building inside of him.

The uncovered tracks screamed "*Trap!*" but it was precisely what Hugh had anticipated when they'd begun their search. Memories of his hellish box flooded his mind, sending a shiver of terror down his spine. Suppressing his instinct to avoid the obvious trap ahead was challenging, but there was no other option to hand.

Hugh turned his mount toward the side road, and Charlotte followed. The surrounding trees blocked out any remaining light in the sky, leaving them in complete darkness. They moved slowly, carefully guiding their mounts down the narrow road. The rain grew heavier, creating a symphony of raindrops against the leaves on the trees around them.

After several minutes of anxious riding, they came upon a clearing. In the centre was an old, dilapidated two-floored building. All its windows on the front facade were dark, but one. Through the window's murky surface, Hugh could see the gentle flicker of firelight from what must have been a low-burning fire.

Beside the building, hidden in the darkness, was a carriage emblazoned with the Reddington family crest.

A surge of anticipation and triumph rushed through him. *This is it.*

He hastily dismounted, his legs aching from their ride, and went to aid Charlotte down from her mare. His hands clasped The Angel's waist, and an untimely wave of desire tingled down his spine. Setting her down, he quickly withdrew and crept toward the carriage.

Glancing about cautiously for any of Reddington's men who might be lurking about, Hugh quietly opened the door of the carriage and searched under the benches for any abandoned weaponry. *Empty.* With a curse, Hugh examined the driver's stoop, and again found nothing.

The heavy rain began to soak through his coat, but he didn't mind the dampness; the warmth from the day still hung in the air and kept him comfortable.

His gaze found Charlotte as she sidled up to the darkened front windows of the building, her bow and an arrow in her hands. Careful not to be seen through the window of the occupied room, Hugh joined Charlotte in her search. He reached her side just as she squinted through another dirty windowpane into a dark room.

She gasped, and Hugh's heart all but stopped.

"What, for God's sake?" he whispered.

"The boys!" She tapped lightly on the glass.

Then Hugh saw them. They sat just beneath the window, against the wall, and their heads both swivelled at the tapping. An orange ball of fluff leapt from Maximus' shoulders, then gave a lazy yawn as it stretched.

The boys' eyes widened. With his heart racing, Hugh quickly gave them the signal for silence, placing his forefinger against his lips. They nodded their understanding and stood, their little faces pale in the faded moonlight.

"*Step back*," Hugh mouthed to them while gesturing with his hands.

They did so.

He trailed his fingers along the edge of the window, searching for weaknesses in the construction. It was not meant to open, but he was certain that with the state of the rest of the building, there ought to be a way to pull it quietly from its sill. Pressing in the bottom corner, he felt some give, and his lips slid sideways in a crooked smile.

Using more force, Hugh pressed again on the weak corner, hoping to dislodge the window further up, as well. All at once, the window shattered with a loud *crash*, the flying shards glittering in the moonlight as they fell to the ground.

Chapter 13

Charlotte's heart lodged in her throat and her stomach sank to her feet as the window shattered. Reddington and his men undoubtedly heard it.

She reached her hand toward her sons, the broken glass notwithstanding. "Hurry, boys. Through the window!"

Maximus bent to scoop up a small orange kitten and put it in his waistcoat, just as a pistol being cocked sounded behind Charlotte. She whirled around, and her heart plummeted. There she stood, staring down the barrel of a pistol.

Hugh sidestepped, placing himself between her and Reddington in a gallant, protective gesture.

"Finally caught up, have you?" Reddington drawled.

Hugh's reply was cut off by Maximus' shrill screech. Charlotte spun around, her breath held in terror at the sight of two men dragging her sons across the small room toward the door.

"*No!*" she cried.

Instinct took over. Charlotte lifted her bow and aimed, drew, and released, sending an arrow deep into one man's shoulder. He howled in agony and staggered, but didn't release Quintin. As quickly as her shot hit its mark, she pulled another arrow from her quiver, strung it on her bow, and drew.

"That is quite enough!" Reddington shouted angrily from behind her. "Drop your weapon."

Her gaze followed her sons as they disappeared through the small room's doorway, anguish all but rending her heart in two, before she turned to face her villainous neighbour.

"Your weapon," he reminded her with a flick of his pistol-wielding wrist.

Grudgingly, Charlotte acquiesced, and placed her bow on the ground at her feet. Would that she could fell the man, retrieve her sons, and be well enough away from Reddington, and Hugh, and all of this dratted nonsense. Her gut twisted painfully, and a lump lodged itself firmly in her throat.

Reddington nodded his satisfaction. "Now, both of you show me your palms."

She and Hugh raised their hands to shoulder height, their palms facing outward.

While she despised facing the end of a pistol, the despair filling her was due to her failure in rescuing her sons. Where were those men taking them? Would they punish the boys for her intervention? Oh, Lord, she hoped that Hugh was right that Reddington wouldn't dare to hurt her boys if he knew it would prevent him from getting what he wanted in the end… Which was *what*, precisely?

"You've successfully lured me here, Reddington," Hugh said, his voice ostensibly calm. "Let Mrs. Bexley and her sons go."

"Not a chance," Reddington sneered. "I do not yet have what I desire."

A warm breeze swept past them, tugging at Charlotte's skirts and chilling the rainwater that soaked her person and the sweat that had formed between her breasts. Despite her eyes having adjusted to the darkness, she could scarcely see anything around her but the blue glow of Reddington's face, half-obscured by his hat and the falling rain, and the dulled grey glint of the pistol.

"And what is it that you desire, Reddington?" Hugh growled.

The blackguard's jaw clenched. "A meeting with your superiors. I need my name cleared and a replacement wife." His leer turned on Charlotte, and his voice lowered to a growl. "If one cannot be provided, I shall *take* one."

A mixture of outrage and fear washed over Charlotte, and she flinched. "I would *never*—"

"I already have your sons; it should not be too difficult to demand more." The bastard shrugged one shoulder.

Hugh stiffened. "The war is over, Reddington. We no longer have reason to be at odds."

Charlotte's heart hiccoughed—*The war is over?*—but fear for her sons swiftly returned as Reddington gripped the pistol tighter and growled.

"The war might be over *for now*," Reddington spat. "But Bonaparte will succeed in the end. In the meantime, I should like a sojourn to the Americas with my wife."

"Why not let Mrs. Bexley and her sons go, and depart for the Americas now? I'm certain that any woman there would find you an amicable match."

Reddington scoffed. "I must be wed before I depart! I—" He growled in frustration. "And I have additional demands that must be met before this lying harlot's sons will be returned."

Charlotte hid a cringe.

"What are your additional demands?" Hugh grunted.

"Lists." Reddington bared his teeth at them. "I want the names of your fellows who have more of Bonaparte's and England's statistical information. I want to know which of *my* fellows are still under investigation. I want—"

Hugh shook his head. "You know very well that I cannot give you any of that information and survive."

Buzzing filled Charlotte's ears as their discussion registered. Charlotte could see only the back of Hugh's head, his ear, and a narrow sliver of the side of his face. But she still stared at him during the exchange with shock, awareness, and…shame weaving through her. Could Hugh have been telling her the truth about his position in the Home Office? *Surely not.*

"Why would Hugh have information that you require?" Charlotte asked, needing to know the truth, at last.

Reddington sneered, his handsome features twisting with hatred and malevolence. "Because your filthy lover is a spy."

Guilt slammed through Charlotte's chest and spread prickling ripples down her arms and back. This was her fault. She'd abandoned Hugh when he needed her; surely Reddington would not have taken her boys if Hugh had been there to protect them. *But he lied!* How could she have *known* that he needed her or that Reddington was a threat? The dratted man hadn't told her the truth of any of it!

Reddington snarled. "Either you forfeit *your* life, or the lives of Bexley's children."

Charlotte's chest squeezed and her stomach roiled as Hugh's jaw clenched.

"A futile threat," Hugh scoffed. "I have already written to my superior and informed him of your involvement with—"

Reddington cursed long and loud over Hugh's words.

"If I go missing," Hugh continued, "he will know that it was at your hands. Your only hope now is to surrender."

A mixture of fury and panic filled Reddington's darkened features, and for a moment the only sound was the rain beating down upon them and the leaves of the trees.

"Give me the bloody information," Reddington snarled, "or I'll take the woman!"

"You couldn't—"

"Aylmer!" Reddington called over his shoulder, careful to not take his gaze from Hugh and Charlotte.

"Aye, your lordship!" a voice called back from somewhere beyond the building.

"Break the big one's arm."

"*Mama*!" Quintin screeched.

"*No!*" Charlotte stepped forward, her heart all but being torn from her chest.

Reddington's lips curved upward. "Hold!"

* * *

The anguish in Charlotte's voice put ice in Hugh's chest.

"I cannot give you what you want, *damn it*!" Hugh exploded. "You know what will happen to you if any harm comes to us…"

For the very briefest of moments, Reddington's focus shifted. In a blink, the man's gaze turned downward, and Hugh acted. He flicked his wrist, forcing the inn's dinner knife into his palm, and threw, all in one swift motion.

Bang! The weapon fired, and Reddington roared in pain as the knife sliced through the back of his pistol-wielding hand. Hugh was vaguely aware of Charlotte's gasp as he ran at Reddington, the spent pistol dropping to the mud-covered ground.

Hugh collided with the bastard, knocking them both down. Pain radiated through Hugh's shoulder on impact, and he gritted his teeth against it. His pulse raced as he wrestled for control over the blackguard. Reddington clawed at Hugh with his bloodied fingers, the edge of the knife stuck in the man's palm tearing at Hugh's clothes. Finally, Hugh gripped Reddington's neck, while his other hand clutched the villain's—and through it, the knife—away from his person as he sat on the man's stomach.

Rainwater sluiced over them, dripping from Hugh's sodden locks and onto Reddington. The heavy raindrops that fell around them from between the trees' leaves splashed in the puddles of their own creation.

Reddington choked, his face turning red as spit bubbled over his purpling lips to be washed away by the rain. "You," he wheezed, "can't…kill me. The boys…will…be killed…if…I don't…make the…rendezvous."

The reminder of Reddington's precautions grated. Hugh scowled, a low growl coming from deep in his chest as he tightened his fingers in one last squeeze before letting go. Reddington gasped and coughed, his face returning to its normal shade of petulant arse. The man might need to remain alive, but Hugh would be damned if he let Reddington resume control over the situation.

Hugh gripped the handle of the inn's knife, and pulled, withdrawing it from Reddington's hand and spraying blood around them to mix with the mud. The man howled hoarsely, holding the injured hand to his chest.

With a look of warning, Hugh rose to his feet and retreated several steps. Charlotte appeared beside him, her bow drawn and an arrow at the ready. The woman was fierce. Hugh admired that about her.

"Tell your men to return my sons," she demanded.

Reddington glowered at them as he stood. "They'll be brought to a safe place," he croaked. "Unless I don't return, of course."

It was subtle, but Hugh noticed the slight dip of Charlotte's shoulders, the tilt to her eyebrows, and the downward curve in the corners of her lips: the telltale sign of powerlessness and fright.

"What do you want now, Reddington?" she asked. "We've established that what you demanded of Hugh cannot be given. What will it now take for you to return my sons?"

Hugh watched Reddington as he awaited the answer. He suspected that he knew what was coming…and that it wouldn't please Charlotte one jot.

He rolled his sodden shoulders, suppressing a cringe at the sharp pain there.

Reddington clenched his jaw, his delicate brow knit in a frown as the warm wind blew at his mud-caked form. "I still want information. But if 'Hugh' cannot provide it, then I demand it from his superior. I want a private meeting with him." His lips thinned as he thought. "He must promise to give me immunity during our rendezvous. I don't want what happened to Lord Hale to happen to me. My neck is not meant for a noose. And I want my bloody bride-to-be back!

Hale promised her to me, and then she ran off. My curst grandmother is withholding my stipend until I marry."

The man was a damned fool. And a coward.

Charlotte opened her mouth to reply, but Hugh cut over her. "Give me four-and-twenty hours, and I will have my superior here to meet with you."

The Angel's shoulders stiffened.

"No tricks!" Reddington pointed a finger at him. "Just your superior. It had better not be a ruse."

"But Hugh," Charlotte began, "my sons! I must ensure their safety—"

"Trust me," Hugh interrupted, his voice carrying as he eyed the blackguard before them. "Reddington knows that if he is to have his demands met he must give the boys proper food, plenty of water, and a comfortable place in which to sleep."

Charlotte spun to glare at her neighbour, her teeth bared in a snarl. "If you so much as harm one single hair on my sons' heads, I will hunt you to the ends of the earth. There is no part of this world that will be safe from me. My arrow will pierce between your eyes so swiftly and quietly—"

"Enough, woman," Reddington grumbled. "Sodding hell. I'll keep your sons safe until I have my meeting with Hugh's superior."

"You will meet me here"—Hugh pointed with the blood-stained knife to the ground at his feet—"in four-and-twenty hours."

Reddington gave another nod, his hand clutched protectively against his stained and soaked waistcoat, and he turned to stride toward his carriage. With some awkward manoeuvring, the men brought the carriage around the back of the building, and Charlotte's eyes flared with panic.

"*I'll come for you, boys*!" she shouted. "Tomorrow, I will have you in my arms again. Do not fear!"

Twin voices of "I love you, Mama!" came from behind the building, and Charlotte's shoulders sagged.

"I love you too, boys!" Her voice croaked, and Hugh found his own throat thickening with emotion.

The *rattle* and *squelch* of carriage wheels on mud faded away, and Charlotte rounded on Hugh. "Four-and-twenty hours? I want my sons *now*! How can I be assured that they will—"

"We will continue this discussion in a more private setting." Hugh glanced through the rain falling around them. Lord knew if

Reddington had any other men lying in wait to listen to their discussion. In all probability, the man was just as he seemed, and his only men were those who had Quintin and Maximus, but Hugh couldn't take that chance.

The Angel stood her ground, stiff, sopping, and furious. "Are you planning something, Hugh? If so, you must tell me at once. I cannot in good conscience trust the well-being of my children to a monster that is capable of such horrific torture. Or have you forgotten that I saw what the man put you through?"

Hugh's still-healing shoulder throbbed at the reminder. "I haven't forgotten," he admitted. "I cannot, however, discuss my plans with you *here*. Come."

With the intent to lead her to their horses, Hugh gently gripped her upper arm. Charlotte's cry of pain halted him in his tracks.

"What the devil?" he muttered, turning his gaze toward her. His heart stopped as he spotted the growing red stain on her arm. "You've been shot!"

Concern jolted through him.

"I have," she muttered. "I believe it's gone right through. And while it pains me, my thoughts remain fixed on my sons."

Her complexion was pallid, but Hugh saw determination there. Having experience in such precarious circumstances before, Hugh knew what their next course of action was. But Charlotte was a complication—a delightful one, but a complication nonetheless. Her emotions were a detriment.

"Can you ride?" he asked over the din of the rain.

The Angel nodded. "I can."

"Very well."

Hugh gritted his teeth as they sloshed through the mud to their mounts. Indeed, Charlotte's close emotional involvement could very likely lead to impulsive—and dangerous—actions that could cost her sons their lives.

Chapter 14

The squish of horses' hooves was scarcely heard over the pounding of the rain. Charlotte curled a sodden lock of hair behind her ear.

They'd been riding in silence for some time, and with every step, Charlotte became more incensed. Hugh had promised to explain his plan in a more private setting, but she had no way of knowing when he would deem their setting private enough.

Her stomach churned, and her heart ached for her sons. Reddington had seemed furious; would he take his anger out on her sons despite Hugh's threats? What was she to do with herself for the next four-and-twenty hours, knowing that her sons were with that horrible man?

Charlotte felt the need to run or scream; her nervous energy was too much to be borne.

"I apologize for my ambiguity earlier," Hugh called through the rain's din. "I could not risk Reddington or his men overhearing my plan."

Finally. Her stomach fluttering, Charlotte waited for him to continue.

"Upon my arrival at the inn this morning, I sent notice to my superior, informing him of my whereabouts and requesting assistance in taking Reddington down. I expect that he—and possibly several of my fellows—will arrive midday tomorrow. We will then have the resources needed to retrieve Quintin and Maximus. Fuck knows we couldn't do it ourselves." He cleared his throat. "Pardon my language. Tonight we must formulate our plan, and tomorrow we will be able to see it through."

"But if these other men join your superior and Reddington in their rendezvous, would Reddington not become irate and…*hurt* my sons?" She swallowed, attempting to push past the lump in her throat.

She cut a sideways glance at him, but could see only the barest milky outline of his shape riding beside her.

"I can assure you that he daren't do any such thing," Hugh said, his voice rumbling. "We *will* get your sons back."

* * *

"Get in and keep yer yaps shut!" one of the bad men shouted.

With a hard shove to his back, Maximus tumbled into a small bedchamber, catching his footing just before he fell. Quintin stumbled beside him, then put a hand to Max's shoulder as they righted themselves.

The door slammed, and Max looked around the dark space. He squinted his eyes in an effort to better see around them. Wedged into the far corner was a bed that would fit one adult, and on the opposite wall was a window looking out into the darkness of night. And there was nothing else.

He swallowed against the lump that had permanently lodged itself in his throat.

Jack squirmed in Max's waistcoat, and he knelt down to let the kitten out. The orange ball of fur stretched his legs and turned to clean himself.

The food they'd been given settled heavily in Maximus' stomach, and he covered the grumbling with his hands.

"At least they fed us," Quin whispered as he knelt to give Jack some food that he'd slipped from his plate earlier.

Max sat on the edge of the room's bed as he watched Quin and Jack in the darkness. The lump in Max's throat got bigger, but swallowing did nothing to make it go away. He sniffed, and the sting of tears burned behind his eyes.

"What do you think happened to Mama?" Max finally voiced the question that had bothered him for the past hours.

Dusting his hands, Quin stood, then moved to sit beside Max on the bed. "Lord Reddington seems right cross, so I think Mama and Hugh bested him."

Another sniff escaped Max, and he scrunched his face in an effort to ward off the tears that threatened. A shiver travelled up his spine at the chill in the air, and he sidled closer to Quintin.

"They *will* find us, Max."

His chest hurt with the force of his sadness, and despite his efforts to hold them back, Max's tears fell.

* * *

Hugh pressed the latch to their bedchamber at the inn and swung the door inward. An elderly maid with drooping eyes stood in the dimly lit corridor, holding a steaming tea service.

"I apologize for ringing so late—again," Hugh whispered.

The woman nodded. "I'm afraid that th' tea isn't as strong as it usually is, as th' cook's to bed and I wasn't certain of the amount for this size of pot."

Hugh shook his head with a smile at the tired maid. "This will be perfect, I'm sure." He accepted the tray and brought it to the writing desk.

"Will you be needing anything else, then, sir?"

He leaned toward the nearby table and lifted a tray covered with an array of mostly used liniments and bandages, shears, a needle and thread, and soiled linens, then handed it to the maid. "We've finished with these items."

She accepted the tray and, with a shallow curtsey, disappeared down the corridor. Hugh closed the door, his hands resting on—and relishing—its warm surface.

As soon as they'd returned from their rendezvous with Reddington, Hugh had set to work stitching the holes in Charlotte's arm. Luckily, the ball had gone right through, so he was not required to retrieve it. Her wound was easily cleaned and closed, but he had been foolish and had kept their sopping clothing on. A chill ran up his spine and gooseflesh prickled his skin, despite the heat from the fire that filled the room.

He turned from the door and looked at The Angel, sitting at the dressing table, her lips blue with cold and her bandaged arm withdrawn from her once-handsome pale-green frock. The garment clung to her other shoulder and draped across her chest and back. It would be difficult now for her to slide her arm from her chemise without tugging at the bandage.

Hugh was a fool, indeed. He'd been so eager to examine her wound that he hadn't given their dripping attire a second thought.

Pressing his chilled lips together in a grim line, he returned to The Angel's side. "Your sodden clothing must be removed," he said, his voice low and calm. "Your body heat will not rise until—"

She surged to her feet, shaking her hands and pacing to expel some energy.

Hugh's chest tightened. "We will get them back, Charlotte." His reassurances sounded hollow even to his own ears, notwithstanding his knowledge that he and his fellows would do everything they could to take Reddington down and safely return Maximus and Quintin to Charlotte.

She nodded, the movement tremulous, then turned sharply to pace back toward him. "I have this—" She huffed a frustrated breath and shook her hands out once more. "I have a need to *move*."

Hugh sat on the foot of the bed, not knowing what to say, while also not wishing to disturb her. So he let her pace.

The hanging material of her frock caught at her hand, and she hissed before tugging fruitlessly at it. "Will you help me…?" She gestured to her frock, and without hesitation, Hugh moved before her.

His fingers trembled as he reached for the buttons at her chest. One by one, the fabric creaked along the small wooden buttons as they gave. Charlotte moved with him, withdrawing her uninjured arm as the dress was opened. Bending, he slid the garment down her legs, pulling the material away from her clinging chemise.

Strong wind blew outside, spraying rain against the windowpane and rattling the frame.

Hugh rose, his stomach buzzing distressingly at her nearness.

"And my stays?" she asked, her voice thick.

The shaking in his fingers grew more intense, and the buzzing in his stomach intensified to an alarming degree. He caught The Angel's gaze, her bright-blue eyes glittering in the firelight. His desire for her was as strong as it was inopportune.

With a harsh mental rebuke, Hugh set to his task. The ties, swollen with water, took several tugs to get loosened, but soon the stays fell away to join the other material on the floor.

"Would you prefer to keep your chemise on?" he asked softly, keeping his gaze steadfastly on her face—and most decidedly *not* on the dusky nipples straining against the front of her chemise.

A shiver wracked her frame and her teeth chattered briefly, but her gaze was direct. "No."

Her dark gaze dropped to his lips, and he knew. He knew with a bone-deep certainty that she needed this. Hell, they *both* did.

Chapter 15

Without allowing herself time to lose her nerve, Charlotte leaned forward and kissed Hugh full on the lips.

Charlotte craved comfort and closeness. She needed to be rid of her nervous energy, to be taken out of herself, out of the worry in her mind and the terror in her heart, if only for a few short moments. And she wanted Hugh to provide such an escape.

She'd been drawn to him from the moment that she'd found him in that rotting structure, but had held herself away. Now, she was done with denying herself what she desired, as long as Hugh would have her.

The memory of their tryst in the kitchen flashed through her mind, and her body warmed further. It had been the first time in Lord knew how long that she'd found completion. And she craved it again now.

His green eyes, darkening with the heat of desire, pierced hers. He smoothed his palm over the base of her neck, tangling his fingers in her loose, damp hair. "I want you, Charlotte."

Her body responded immediately, a flood of need rushing to her core, her pulse speeding, and gooseflesh spreading over her skin.

"I want you, too," she confessed.

With a low growl and careful—if frenzied—movements, Hugh helped her free of her chemise then peeled the sopping clothes from himself, until they stood nude. His body was partially obscured by shadows, the ripple of firelight highlighting the curve of his bottom and the toned ridges of his arm, waist, and thigh. She shivered, and Hugh's eyes darkened.

"Come, we will warm ourselves in bed."

She accepted his hand and curled between the bedclothes, sidling close to his body and relishing the feel of his skin against hers. Need swept through her, and she clung to him, taking his lips in another kiss and pressing herself closer to him.

Despite his *very* evident desire for her, his kiss was languid and measured. Gooseflesh spread across Charlotte's skin, and her stomach quivered with anticipation of what was to come.

His tongue playfully flicked hers, and her pulse leapt. Her sense of urgency and her intense desire to feel the heat of him took over. Suddenly too hot, she lowered the bedclothes to her thighs. Shock rippled through her at her own daring, but she refused to be bashful. Hugh's gaze turned wide as he took in her nude body through the dimness.

Charlotte was certain that he could not see very much, but it was enough for her to wonder if he saw her flaws. Did he notice the scars that reached from her hips to her stomach? The small brown spot that had made a home above her belly button? *And what of my breasts?* She nearly covered them with her arms; they'd begun to droop after the births of her sons, and the skin around her areolae had grown and darkened.

Her confidence waned further when he placed his hands on her skin and began to explore. He fingered the marks and scars that marred her otherwise smooth skin before he traced the curve of her waist and cupped her breasts.

The knowledge that she didn't have her younger body, despite her still-youthful age, had heretofore never felt so obvious.

Hugh must have sensed her wavering certainty, for his heated gaze rose to meet hers. "You…" he began, then cleared his throat. "You are perfect."

Her heart soared. She knew that it couldn't possibly be true, but that he thought her worth the compliment was heartening. Fighting against the sting at the back of her eyes, Charlotte bent to take his lips once more. His words pierced her right through the heart. Never, in all her life, had she heard a sentence that felt so akin to a balm upon an opened wound.

"Thank you," she whispered against his lips.

Heart racing, she reached for the bedclothes covering Hugh. "I want to see you, too."

His gaze glittering in the dimness, Hugh slid the bedclothes down to his waist, then kicked the cloth away.

Hugh clasped her waist and silently urged her over top of him, her legs straddling him. A fresh surge of desire swept through her. Her stomach fluttering, Charlotte traced her hands over Hugh's chest. His skin was still cool to the touch, and she was careful not to apply too much pressure to his still-healing wounds, but *my*, his body was fine, indeed.

Many of the scars on his skin were still pink and rippled, while others had long turned white. The yellowed bruising on his shoulder drew her gaze, and she leaned forward to scatter kisses there. He hissed a breath as the motion pressed her *mons* to the ridge of his erection, teasing them both. Her body responded with a heavy throb.

Hugh's jaw was clenched, his eyes half-lidded, and his chest rose and fell swiftly with each breath. She was buoyed by the knowledge that Hugh wanted her just as much as she wanted him.

The need to ride him until she found her fulfilment was strong, but more than satiating her lust, Charlotte wanted to explore him, to satisfy her curiosity about him…to *taste* him.

A smile spread over her lips as she slid down the bed.

"What are you—"

She shushed him with a finger to her lips.

Knowing what it took for a man to slide easily into a woman's passage, she bent over his cooled legs and took his erection into her mouth.

A sharp gasp escaped Hugh. "*Charlotte!*" He cursed under his breath. "Bloody hell, what are…you… Good God, that…" His words trailed away into a groan as she took him deeper into her mouth and applied some suction.

His body twitched, and he groaned again.

He was smooth and heavy, with the faint salty taste that she remembered men had. Just the scent of him in her nose and the taste of him on her tongue sent a fresh wave of molten heat to her core. She *needed* him.

"Charlotte, I… Hell, I'm not…going to last…"

With one final lap of his shaft and tip, Charlotte rose to straddle him once more, carefully guiding him to her opening.

Hugh panted as he gripped her waist, his eyes entirely glazed over with lust. "Charlotte…"

Slowly, she lowered herself, gradually sinking further and further over him and relishing the feel of him inside her once more. Hugh pressed back against the pillow, his jaw taut and his neck red and straining.

"*Hell's teeth, Charlotte.*"

Her body accepted him with a willing tightness, one bit at a time, until he was—at *last*—fully sheathed.

A faint sheen of sweat coated her skin, and her heart pumped a staccato beat against her ribs.

Instinct and desire driving her, she lifted up slightly on her knees and slid back down. Unbidden, a moan escaped her. *More*, her body urged. No matter how much she'd wanted to explore him, her need was heightened to a painful degree.

She did it again, and again, eliciting yet more erotic cries from her lips.

Hugh's hands tightened on her hips, and she leaned forward, putting her hands to either side of his head and pressing her breasts to his chest. There was a twinge in her injured arm, but she steadfastly ignored it. The change in position brought her folds in contact with the curling hairs above his member, and the light graze sent delightful quivers through her abdomen. It proved a rather addictive sensation.

Chasing that feeling, and knowing that she was growing close, she rocked her pelvis back and forth. A shudder shook her as a fresh, new wave of delight took over. "That feels…so…" she gasped.

"Yes, Angel," Hugh moaned. "Yes, it…does."

He wrapped his arms around her, one about her hips and one at her shoulders, his hand sliding through her hair and against the base of her head as he took her lips with his.

Charlotte continued rocking. The gentle abrasion on her folds, the rubbing of her nipples against his chest, and the sensation of his tongue tangling with hers combined to wind her body so tightly in a coil she knew she would soon burst. The more she moved, the tighter she wound, the pressure building.

Her breath came in rapid bursts. Sparks ignited just beneath her skin, her body taut with pressure. She moved, riding him faster, winding herself tighter until, finally, she burst.

Light exploded behind her eyelids, and her body shook with the force of her completion, her cry called to the ceiling as her head dropped back. She continued to move her hips, riding the waves of passion that crashed through her.

Chapter 16

Watching The Angel find her completion was like nothing Hugh had ever experienced. It brought him more pride, more joy, than he'd ever thought possible. Hell, he could have ended the encounter now and felt satisfied.

But he wouldn't.

Charlotte continued to ride him, her sweet sheath pulsing with the waves of her completion. His heart thundered in his ears as he held her close. He wanted to finish inside her, but couldn't risk it without the barrier of a cundum.

She moaned again, and Hugh grit his teeth. He couldn't hold himself off any longer.

With one last rock of her hips, he gripped her bottom and lifted, pulling his hips back and freeing his cock from her heat just in time. A deep growl rose from his chest as he spilled his seed, the warm, white stickiness streaming over his abdomen as he came.

His eyes closed, Hugh dropped his head back against the pillow. His raspy breath came rapidly as his mind lowered from the clouds.

"By God, Charlotte."

She laughed breathily and shifted herself to lie beside him. "I feel the same way."

Now that his ears weren't filled with the pounding of his own heart and The Angel's cries of delight, he could hear the wind and rain further rattling the bedchamber's window.

"My arm throbs," she noted sleepily.

He pressed a kiss to her forehead. "I'm sorry," he replied. "Rest."

Hell's teeth, but two times with Charlotte was not enough. He knew already that he wanted to take her to bed again—though he would wait until after they'd retrieved her sons.

The reminder of their task sent a pang through his chest as his worry returned.

With a regretful sigh, he pressed a hand to the air-chilled mess on his abdomen and rose from the bed, striding to the washbasin to clean himself off. Water sloshed as he dunked a cloth in, then wiped at his skin.

At some point the next day, his fellows—at least a pair of them, Hugh hoped—would arrive to aid them in the rescue. If Hydra himself didn't join them, one of the others might be required to put on a show and pretend to be his superior. Hugh just hoped that Reddington hadn't seen Sir Charles Bradley before, and would believe their ruse.

Having finished his ablutions, Hugh turned toward the bed, and stilled. Charlotte reclined on the bed with the blanket tucked about her shoulders, her eyes fixed on him, warm and inviting.

The bedclothes were cool against his flushed skin; he drew them up over his chest, lying on his back.

That was remarkable. *Charlotte* was remarkable. Her body, while lithe and slender, was marked with the proof of her motherhood; he'd not seen that the first time they'd made love, but he felt honoured to have seen it now. Hell if he could explain it, but Hugh found it damned attractive. He admired her strength and will, her determination and perseverance.

Sex with Charlotte was far…*more* than it had been with any other woman, and yet he hadn't quite figured out why.

"I apologize for not believing you earlier."

His chest warmed. "You needn't apologize, but it is appreciated, nonetheless. It is an unbelievable truth, to be sure."

"Difficult to believe or not," she uttered sleepily to the ceiling, "I have a tenacious mistrust of men. I ought to have listened when you spoke, instead of dismissing your words as falsehoods."

His gaze sharpened on her. "Whyever would you mistrust men?" he asked. "What happened?"

The Angel's face twisted in pain before she shook her head. "I would prefer not to elaborate, if you do not mind."

Anger ignited in his gut at the man—or *men*—who had contributed to her pain, but even as the feeling registered, he recognized that he himself had added to her pain. Guilt swiftly joined his anger, and he cleared his throat against it. "Of course."

"What is it that you do as a spy…if you are at liberty to say?" she asked, apparently eager for a change in subject.

She shifted on the bed, sidling closer to Hugh. In silent understanding, Hugh wrapped an arm about her shoulders, pulling her against his ribs with a sigh.

"My main position is as a tail," he rumbled, "but I often perform other duties, as well."

She pulled her lip between her teeth. "You were following Reddington?"

He swallowed. "I was, yes."

* * *

Charlotte's stomach tightened. That meant that Reddington was already a person of interest to the Secret Service before Hugh had been tasked with following him. What *else* had the man done?

"I imagine that my superior will have many questions when he arrives," Hugh continued.

"You will have quite the tale to tell," Charlotte added.

He huffed a breath. "Indeed."

"How did you come to be a spy?" she asked, her curiosity piqued.

Hugh was silent for a few short heartbeats as he considered her question. "When Philip and I—"

"Philip?" She lifted her head to gaze down into his solemn green eyes. "Who is that?"

"My brother."

Realization rattled through her that this was yet another layer of his deceit. At the moment, however, she couldn't allow it to affect her. This had been the longest day of her life, and while she mightn't feel that she could fully trust the man in her arms yet, she needed the comfort that he offered.

"Very well. Please continue."

His lips pursed, and he nodded as she settled back down upon his chest.

"When we were young, our parents were murdered—"

"Oh, how awful," she breathed. "I'm so sorry."

"Thank you." He cleared his throat once more. "I recklessly followed the culprit and found myself in a…difficult situation. That was when Theophilus Samuels, the Viscount Leeds, rescued me. He brought Philip and me into his home and his school."

"Lord Leeds raised you both to be spies?"

Hugh shook his head. "Only I chose to continue on. My brother was schooled, but he elected not to enter into service. It is not mandatory, you see. These men—these *great* men—rescued urchins off the streets of St. Giles and gave them food, housing, and an education. It was the student's choice whether they wanted to serve England in return. While many chose not to, however, they are still allies. If any of our men requires aid or a safe house, they are always welcome to seek out their fellow students, and they will be aided without hesitation."

Another gust of wind and rain shook the window, and Charlotte nestled deeper into the crook of Hugh's arm.

"Does Lord Leeds continue to find urchins?" she asked.

"I'm afraid not," he said quietly. "Lord Leeds passed on several years ago now, and his son, Christian Samuels, has inherited the title. But my superior, called Hydra, and his equals—Hades, Ares, and Hermes—still find and train young people in need."

They sat in silence for several long moments, the rain, the wind, the flickering fire, and their measured breathing the only sounds filling the room.

"We were treated as a family," Hugh finally said.

"By whom?" she asked drowsily.

"By our superiors, and among my fellows and me. Many of us are within five years of one another, while the younger men and women are fresh out of training."

"Indeed? Sounds lovely."

He tightened his hold on her shoulders. "It was. I not only developed strong, lasting friendships with them, but also formed a brother and sisterhood. I miss them dreadfully. Gabe, Colin, Stevens, Barrows…"

"Will they arrive on the morrow, do you suppose?"

Hugh shook his head. "I'm unsure. But we must prepare for a discussion with them regarding our plans."

"Thank you…for attempting to protect my sons. And me."

"You're welcome." He looked down at her, his gaze warm but staid. "I promise that I will never lie to you again, Charlotte."

More warmth spread over her chest, and she cautiously accepted the feeling. He seemed to believe his promise, and the help and honesty that he was currently offering was a balm to her jaded views.

She nodded, her eyes dipping with exhaustion as she covered a yawn.

"I'd thought—" He shifted, tilting his head so that he could look into her eyes. "You're tired," he noted.

Charlotte smiled up at him. "You can keep talking. I like the sound of your voice."

Huffing a short laugh, he settled back against the bed, his arm snug against her shoulders.

Her arm throbbed with the beat of her aching heart, and her stomach still twisted uneasily. Hugh's discussion was an adequate distraction, but her body still knew that something was wrong.

She licked her drying lips. "Tell me that everything is going to be well again," she whispered.

Hugh replied without hesitation. "Everything will be well again." He pressed a kiss to the top of her head, sending tingles of awareness through her. "I promise, Charlotte, that I will get your sons back or die trying."

Nerves tingled just beneath her skin in a skittering wave. "I've already saved your life once before, Hugh," she replied flippantly. "Pray do not make me do so again."

He pressed a kiss to her cheek, her jaw, and, finally, her lips, and her body veritably purred.

With a hum of contentment, she turned in his arms, facing away from him. Hugh positioned himself against her back. They lay like spoons would sit in a drawer, his spent cock nestled snugly against the crease of her bottom.

Gratification thrummed through her body as she settled into a deep sleep, enveloped in Hugh's warmth.

* * *

Hugh slowly came awake, the grey light of the morning brightening the rain clouds outside the window. He blinked, memories of the night prior flooding his mind. His body came instantly awake, and he turned his gaze toward his bedmate. Charlotte lay beside him, her expression soft as she slept.

He hated that she'd experienced pain. It was Hugh's fault, blast it. *He* was the one who had kept quiet about the possibility of danger when he'd been recovering. It was *he* who had evaded her polite inquiries about his identity and lied when compelled to reply. It was foolish to think that he could have protected her by avoiding the truth.

Guilt churned in his gut, as it had for most of the day prior and throughout the night. Hell if he knew what to do about Charlotte. He couldn't stomach the fact that she'd been shot, and just the thought that it could happen again sent him into an unfamiliar—and entirely alarming—panic.

A light rain sprayed the window, drawing Hugh's attention. The roads would be muddy rivers by now. It was unseasonably wet for early July; he hoped that the sun would show itself to dry the rain for the rendezvous that evening.

He must convince Charlotte to agree to a plan that put her in less danger. Mayhap she could remain back with the horses or hidden in a carriage while Hugh and his fellows arranged for the retrieval of her sons.

With a sigh and a gentle nudge, he prodded Charlotte's shoulder. "We must awaken. Our plan must be formulated."

Her eyes snapped open, and she sat upright, the bedclothes falling to her waist and revealing her glorious breasts in the full light of the room. He gasped despite himself and then coughed in a small choke. *Christ*, but Hugh very nearly swallowed his tongue.

"We must plan for the rendezvous," he repeated.

"Yes." She rubbed at her face and curled her hair behind her ears. "Of course."

With swift movements, they donned their dried clothing and sat upon the chaise before the fire.

"What if your superior gave Reddington precisely what he requests?"

Hugh's spine stiffened in surprise, and he turned his disbelieving gaze on her. "Give him information about the Secret Service, a pardon, a sodding *wife*, and passage to the Americas?"

Charlotte shrugged one shoulder. "Mayhap—"

"Impossible! Reddington will not rest until he has *all* that he—"

Her gaze narrowed. "If it sees my sons returned to me, I—"

"I daresay my superior will have something to say on the matter."

She growled in frustration. "Then I shall make known to your superior my feelings on this matter."

Hugh jutted his chin. "I do not think that is wise."

She surged to her feet and placed her fists upon her waist, her face mutinous. "My sons are being held captive by a man capable of—" Her lips twisted. "I do not care how many treasonous acts the man has committed, Hugh, I would see the man given everything that he desires, and more, if it meant that my sons would be returned to me safely!"

A nervous shudder swelled in Hugh's abdomen. The Angel had every right to feel this way, of course, but any deviation from their plan could be a *detriment* to her sons' safety. And hers. His gaze caught on the bloodstained sleeve of her frock, and his heart clenched. He didn't wish to risk it if there was another way. "Perhaps it would be best if you remained here during the meeting. You would be safe, and I would ensure—"

"*What?*" she breathed.

* * *

Charlotte might very well choke on the pain lancing through her. Lord, she'd been shot last evening, but *this* hurt far more. Betrayal. *Again.*

She dropped her head to her hands, shame and regret washing over her, knotting her stomach and twisting in her chest. "I cannot believe that I allowed myself to be deceived once more." She groaned into her hands. "What a fool I was to let desire rule my head…*again!*"

"I only suggest it for your safety, Charlotte," the cad said.

Her head snapped up as anger swiftly replaced her self-reproach.

"What of my *sons'* safety, Hugh? What of their need for their mother?"

"If I did not have to worry over your safety, I could better focus my attentions on retrieving your sons." He spread his hands in apparent innocence.

Another slash of pain sliced through her chest. "I am a burden… I see."

"You are not a burden, Char—"

"Ah, but you are making it very clear that I am," she interrupted, the startling pain in her chest growing stronger. "You are only here because I thought I could trust you to *help me*, not to shut me out of your plans."

"I *do* intend to help you."

"Well, you had best begin to think of this *burden* as a proverbial barnacle on your ship until my sons are retrieved." She swallowed past the sudden lump that had formed in her throat. "Once I have them back at home, you may deal with Reddington as you will, and never see me again."

Something flashed across Hugh's face, but it was gone before Charlotte could decipher it. He strode forward and reached for her hand, but she pulled it away.

With a nod and a grim smile, he stepped back. "I apologize, Charlotte. I didn't intend to hurt you. Only to protect you from further injury."

Her pulse raced with anger and hurt, making her entire body throb.

"Call me Mrs. Bexley, if you please." She swallowed again and opened her mouth to speak, but loud male voices coming from belowstairs stopped her. They weren't shouting, but, goodness, they were certainly a loud group.

Hugh took another retreating step. "I believe that is for us." His voice was low, and his countenance was dour. "I will go belowstairs to greet them."

"You mustn't leave without me," she warned.

He nodded once. "I will await you in the taproom…Mrs. Bexley."

Charlotte stood tall, her shoulders back, and forced self-assuredness on her features as Hugh quit the room. She wanted to crumple, to fling herself to the bed where they'd made love only the night before, and weep, but she didn't. She *couldn't*. Instead, she strode resolutely to the dressing table and began to fix her hair. Her sons were waiting for her, and she was determined to be a part of the planning for their rescue, no matter what notions Hugh had.

Chapter 17

"*Hugh*!" Hydra's exclamation was a balm to the ache in Hugh's chest.

Hugh trod down the last step of the stairs to the taproom, and he was surrounded by four of his fellows and his superior.

"By God, man, what the devil are you wearing?" one of his best and oldest friends, Colin Greene, exclaimed jovially.

"Where have you been?" Thomson asked.

"Are you injured?" McCully eyed Hugh's person.

Hydra brushed the others aside. "Perhaps we ought to sit down."

Colin, McCully, Thomson, and Brown led the way toward a dining table in the far left corner, which sat secluded from the rest of the taproom.

"We have much to discuss," Hydra muttered from beside Hugh.

Hugh nodded. "I know, sir."

His superior put his hand on Hugh's uninjured shoulder. "We've all been very worried about you, Hugh," he said, his gaze searching. "Are you *truly* well?"

Hugh returned Hydra's gaze, but in his mind's eye, he saw Charlotte—*Mrs. Bexley*. It had hurt a far sight more than he would have expected when she'd placed that emotional barrier between them once more. Their association had finally grown comfortable, and he'd gone and burned himself. The pain written on her features had crushed him.

He cleared his throat and forced a wan smile. "My wounds are healing."

"When we'd learned that you were in a small outbuilding on Reddington's land, we set out directly," Hydra said in a rough whisper. "I saw the place, Hugh… It must have been a nightmare."

Closing his eyes against the concern and pity on his superior's face, Hugh nodded. Indeed, it had been a nightmare. One that he daren't think on overmuch. "Yes, sir."

"Are you comfortable giving a briefing to the group?"

Hugh nodded again. "Of course."

Hydra clapped him lightly on the back. "Come on, then."

Hugh kept his back to the wall so that he would spot Charlo—Mrs. Bexley—when she entered.

Without preamble, Hugh recounted the events of the previous two months. He began with his misadventure tailing Reddington and ended with the failed rescue of the evening before. During his speech, a barmaid delivered ale to the men, but all of them abstained.

The men were quiet for several long moments before Brown broke the silence. "Blimey."

"I'm glad that Mrs. Bexley found you," McCully said. "I've been searching for you for some time, and was near to giving up hope."

"You look like one of Astley's performers." Colin grinned at him, but the smile failed to reach his eyes.

Hydra cast a sharp glance at Colin. "Have a care, Greene; they're borrowed." He turned back to Hugh. "When you sent your missive, I happened to be at the school visiting Samuels and his wife, and our seamstress informed me that she had two suits of clothes saved from your last visit. I've brought them with us."

"Thank you, sir. Samuels is *married?*" Hugh's eyebrows jumped upward as shock jolted through him. Christian Samuels was the Secret Service's most skilled cryptologist, and his mentor Lord Leeds' son.

"Indeed he is," Hydra confirmed. "And recovering nicely."

A frown crossed Hugh's brow. "Recovering?"

"Samuels and his wife helped to capture a traitor to the Crown, but in the process, Samuels was gravely injured. Dr. Stainton treated his wounds, and he is recovering at the school."

"Ah." Hugh nodded. He'd missed a fair amount of activity in his absence. "What else is new with our fellows?"

"Barrows remains unconscious at the safe house in London," McCully offered. "Was knocked on the back of the head."

"That's dreadful."

Brown nodded. "Richards went missing, and we've been searching for him, as well. We have a whole group of our new students spread out over the countryside."

"Callum and Harris are on assignment, chasing one of Reddington's compatriots on the ocean." Hydra grinned.

Colin chuckled. "Get to be bloody pirates."

Hugh grinned. "Callum's dream has finally been realized, then."

"Aye." Hydra nodded. "I daresay they will enjoy the assignment a sight more than they ought. But with the war ended, mayhap it was precisely what they required."

"So much will change now," Brown put in. "Many intend to become Runners. Including Lucy—who has now claimed the name Grace. As I understand it, she is to begin a Bow Street office full of women, doing work *for* women."

Hugh grinned, picturing the shapely woman with brown hair and piercing grey-green eyes who had always been willing to put in hard work and was fiercely concerned about the welfare of women. He could well imagine her taking on a business venture on her own. "An ideal position for her, indeed."

He cleared his throat. "How fares Gabe?" Gabriel Ashley was the closest friend of Hugh and Colin. The three of them developed a fast friendship when they started their spy education at the school in Brampton.

"He's Baron Winning now," Colin replied.

His eyebrows lifting to his hairline, Hugh cursed.

"Indeed," Colin muttered. "His cousin, Frederick, was shot in cold blood. Gabe, Mary, and I witnessed it while observing a clandestine rendezvous between Napoleon's spies."

"Bloody hell." Hugh pinched the bridge of his nose. *Poor Gabe.*

Colin cleared his throat. "He's to be married."

"*Pardon*?" Hugh's head snapped up. "*Gabe* is to be married?"

His friend grinned.

Hugh returned his smile. "By damn! He finally did it."

"I said as much to him the last we spoke. He's been in love with Mary since childhood; I'm surprised it's taken him so bloody long to realize it."

"Stevens is to be married, as well," Hydra put in. "His fiancée is the sister of Samuels' new wife."

"Capital!" While Hugh was pleased for his friends, a part of him felt sorrow for having missed so many life events.

Christ, but many of his friends, it seemed, had found love and would be able to settle down now that the war was over. Would that Hugh could boast the same. At that moment, he hadn't even a notion of what would come for him, his future entirely uncertain. Despite himself, a quiver of nerves started low in his belly.

Movement toward the taproom's stairs caught his eye, and he looked up to see *Mrs. Bexley* striding toward them. Hugh stood, and his fellows followed suit.

Her pale-green frock was wrinkled and stained, but she still looked radiant. Her hair was plaited and wrapped into a tight bun at her crown. Hugh had the sudden—and intense—urge to pull it free and fan it over her shoulders. Or a pillow. She neared them, smiling grimly in greeting at the other men and pointedly avoiding eye contact with Hugh.

Guilt hit him anew, tingling in his fingertips and racing along his arms and chest. *Damnation.*

"Mrs. Bexley." He gestured toward the men. "This is my superior, Sir Charles Bradley—or Hydra. These fine men are my fellows: Mr. Greene, Mr. McCully, Mr. Brown, and Mr. Thomson."

She exchanged pleasantries, then stopped at Colin and Brown. "I've met you both before. You came to my home in search of Hugh."

Shock rippled through Hugh, his heart giving a hard *thump.* "They *what?*"

She nodded. "Just after Lord Reddington came to question me, and you departed." She turned to the two men. "I'm sorry. I did not know who you were to him."

The men replied, but the words were entirely lost on Hugh, his ears instead filled with the rush of his pulse. They took their seats—*Mrs. Bexley* across from Hugh—while his mind reeled. Had he remained a mere few moments longer, he would have been reunited with his fellows, and he would have been better able to protect her and her sons. He could have lured Reddington away, he could have— *Christ,* but everything might be different now…

Hydra leaned forward in his seat and spoke in an undertone. "Hugh has informed us of the events of last evening. From what I surmise, Lord Reddington is aware of his dire circumstances and cravenly wishes to barter for his freedom with the lives of two innocent children." The men listened intently to their leader. "We require a plan."

* * *

"The man's a fool," one of the men—Mr. Thomson?—said dismissively.

"A dangerous fool," Hugh countered.

Mr. Thomson shook his head. "Dangerous, yes. But surely he would not think to search the forest around the meeting place or feel for weaponry on Hugh and Hydra?"

The men had been discussing their plans for rescuing her sons for a quarter of an hour, and Charlotte had had enough.

"If," she broke into the hushed discussion, "the man is such a fool, how had he known to capture Hugh from the start? How had he known that Hugh was in my home, and that by taking my boys he would see a result? The man might be a fool in some respect, but I imagine him entirely capable of understanding deceit, and seeing through your feeble web."

Hugh let out a soft groan, while Hydra gazed at her with curiosity.

"Have you adjustments to our plan in mind, Mrs. Bexley?" Hydra asked.

Refusing to meet Hugh's insistent gaze, she kept hers steady on his superior. "Give him what he wants." The men burst into a low chatter, but she cut over them. "The war is over; offer him lists that no longer matter—"

"All of our lists are in code, and giving the man anything in our code would be akin to giving him our cipher," Hydra put in. "That would be dangerous, indeed."

A sob caught in her throat, but she swallowed it back. "But I *must* get my sons back…"

The man nodded. "We will do everything in our power to make that happen. So while we appreciate your input, Mrs. Bexley, that plan is just not possible."

The men continued their discussion, and she was shut out with a finality that made her heart sink and her stomach swoop with nerves and fear. Men were entirely unreliable, and infuriatingly unwilling to listen to a perfectly judicious plan. They needn't use their *actual* lists. Indeed, they could simply write lists of names or places, and claim that they have importance. Finding a woman who would agree to a scheme would be simple enough—sod it, *Charlotte* could be that woman! They could then simply make Lord Reddington *believe* that they were carrying out the exchange, and then capture the man once she had her sons returned to her.

Soon, the men's discussion turned to other topics, and fare was brought to the table.

Charlotte's eyes glazed over as she stared at the plate of food before her. She'd lost interest once they'd switched to the agriculture of one man's bit of land. Her mind was rather consumed with her sons—and rightfully so, blast it.

She slid her gaze over the men at the table. Hugh had some handsome friends, she would grudgingly admit, and with a pang of guilt, noted again Mr. Greene and Mr. Brown as the men who had come in search of Hugh at her house. Her guilt deepened as she recalled the falsehood that she'd told them. She detested lying, but surely if it was for Hugh's protection, it was acceptable?

Her blood ran cold and her fingers began to tremble. That's what *Hugh* had done, wasn't it? He'd lied in an effort to keep her safe.

She swallowed back a groan and resisted the urge to hide her face in her hands. How had she not seen it before? He'd lied to *protect* her, whereas her husband's lies had always been for his own gain or pleasure.

Guilt welled up so much she feared that she might choke. *Hell.* She needed to think on this further, but now, she had to focus on her sons and the men's plan to retrieve them.

Her gaze turned toward Hugh. The man had implied that she was a burden, so while she mightn't hold anger toward him regarding his lies, he *had* more recently hurt her… He shook his head and pointed his fork at another man at the table, and whispered something in reply. Others responded, and back and forth it went, while they all consumed their meals.

Charlotte had no appetite. She knew, however, that she required nourishment for the evening ahead, so she forced herself to eat several bites of the dry, flavourless beef. It sat like a stone in her stomach as dread plagued her.

A chair scraped against the wooden floor as Hydra stood, dabbing his lips with a tattered napkin. "I intend to prepare my arsenal, and I suggest that the rest of you do so, as well." He leaned forward, placing his palms on the table and piercing his men with his impassioned blue gaze. "You'd best remember that while Reddington is a fool and a coward, he is impetuous. A very dangerous man."

The others nodded their understanding.

Dangerous, indeed, Charlotte mused. The man was a monster…and he had her sons.

* * *

The rain had begun again, chilling Charlotte as it seeped into her ruined green frock. Leela's strong muscles moved beneath her, her hooves struggling for grip on the muddy road.

"Here!" Hugh called back to the men who followed, pointing ahead to the hidden side road that led to their meeting spot.

Charlotte pulled on Leela's reins, slowing to a gradual stop. The others swiftly followed suit. Heavy breathing, the horses' snorts, and the spattering of rain on leaves and mud sounded loud to Charlotte's ears. In order to avoid detection, they were early for the scheduled rendezvous between the man called Hydra and Reddington. And she was nervous.

"This is where we part, men," Hydra announced. "You know what to do."

Before Charlotte could turn and ride into the forest with the other men, Hugh stopped her. He pulled Percy up beside Leela, then raked his fingers through his wet hair.

The man was devastatingly handsome in his own clothes, wet though they were. He wore a pair of brown riding breeches and a coat of the same colour, both matching the exact shade of his hair when it was wet. His waistcoat was burgundy, which set his green eyes to sparkling, and his shirt and cravat were cream. Hugh's bruising had faded even more, but his scars still stood out against the colour of his skin.

"Will you be well, Char—Mrs. Bexley?" he asked over the din of the rain.

A distasteful quiver spread over her chest at the sound of her married name on his lips, and she raised her chin a notch in response. "You needn't concern yourself with me; I shall be fine, as long as my sons are returned to me."

His lips thinned and his jaw clenched, but with a shuddering nod, he turned Percy and rode after his superior.

"Mrs. Bexley?" A voice came from behind her.

Charlotte, adjusting the bow and quiver slung across her back, turned to face Mr. Thomson. "I'm coming." She started forward, falling into place beside the man.

"I vow we will do everything in our power to retrieve your sons," he said softly, just scarcely audible over the rain.

Her eyes burned, and she quickly blinked back her tears. "Yes," she managed. "Thank you."

They walked their mounts into the forest, following the general direction of the others. Charlotte brushed aside a branch, then another, water droplets falling on her from the leaves.

"Hydra is a good man," Mr. Thomson said. "I've known him for years. Has his own child, newly born."

"I am pleased for him."

Thomson nodded. "Indeed, I believe he understands the connection that a parent can have with a bairn." He glanced at her and sighed. "I apologize, Mrs. Bexley. I know this is difficult."

Charlotte attempted to clear her throat of the lump that had lodged there, but failed. "Thank you," she croaked.

Chapter 18

The distant rumble and slosh of horses' hooves alerted Hugh to Reddington's impending presence. Hugh's spine stiffened as he shifted his booted feet in the mud. He slid a glance toward Hydra, whose gaze was fixed ahead. He'd heard the horses, as well, then.

Their mounts grazed uneasily under the shelter of a nearby tree, backs slick with water.

Hugh scanned the treeline, wondering how far back Charlotte and his fellows had hidden. Would they be able to hear the exchange? How was Charlotte feeling? He imagined that she would be terrified.

You needn't concern yourself with me; I shall be fine. Her words rang through his mind, and he ground his teeth against the ache that throbbed in his chest. What was wrong with him? Never had a woman's words or emotions so affected him, most particularly while he was performing his duties. But Charlotte—*damnation*—Mrs. Bexley was different. He had the profound urge to earn her trust and ensure her happiness.

The noise grew louder, and soon a carriage came into view, pulling Hugh back to the moment. His heart thundered in his ears as the wheels rolled to a halt and Reddington disembarked, the two children and one injured man following from inside. The driver leapt down from his perch and followed Reddington toward Hugh.

"I expected only your superior to be here, Hugh," Reddington drawled.

Hugh clenched his jaw in an effort to stop himself from uttering a curt remark. "He would not have known where to meet with you had I not joined him."

Reddington twisted his lips in thought before grunting. "Very well."

The rain slowed to a light mist that was carried on the wind. A hard gust blew, sending a chill up Hugh's spine.

"I understand that those boys are Mrs. Bexley's children." Hydra stepped forward. "It has been requested that I return them to their mother. If you wish to speak with me, I would suggest that we begin and conclude our business swiftly so that I might make good on my promise."

Reddington motioned toward his men, and they nudged the boys forward. Hugh's heart nigh stopped at the sight of them as they neared. Poor Maximus had tears streaked down his dirt-stained cheeks. The boys must be petrified.

"What is it that you want from me in exchange for the boys?" Hydra asked.

"Protection from the noose, firstly. Then, I require lists, *information*—"

Hydra clucked his tongue. "You have done many a terrible thing, Lord Reddington. How do you propose that I protect you?"

"You know damned well how!" Reddington spat. "And I want the wife that was promised to me."

With a shake of his head, Hydra replied, "The woman that you had been 'promised' is already spoken for. She was married weeks ago."

"*Horseshit*!" Reddington's cheeks grew ruddy with rage. "Violet Wilkinson was *mine*! I paid for her, damn it!" His jaw bulged as he clenched it. "I demand another woman, then. Someone with whom I might start a life in the Americas."

* * *

Charlotte tilted her head in a fruitless attempt to hear the exchange. Reddington gestured angrily, and Hydra said something soothingly.

"I *demand*..." Reddington's voice softened, and Charlotte could not hear the rest of his words.

She sighed in frustration. They'd settled in a spot unnecessarily far from the clearing; she wished that they'd better chosen. If they'd had a better vantage point, she could have taken the cads down with her bow and been done with it.

She stifled a groan. Her legs ached from being so long in their crouched position; she'd lost the feeling of the bottom half entirely.

"It will be well, Mrs. Bexley," Mr. Thomson said in an undertone from directly beside her, crouched in the brush. "Hydra knows well how to negotiate."

Her gaze slid back to her sons, and her heart tripped over in her chest. They were frightened, and it tore her apart. Her body shook with the need to hold them in her arms, painful prickles of fear spreading out all over. These men had better work swiftly, for she couldn't go much longer without her boys.

"I certainly hope so, Mr. Thom—"

A blinding flash of lightning lit the air around them, followed closely by the deafening *boom* of thunder. Their horses whinnied, rearing up on their hind legs. Charlotte cringed, only just resisting the urge to cry out in alarm.

Reddington shouted profanities and withdrew two pistols from within his coat. "*Who is out there?*" he screeched. "Show yourself!"

Charlotte stood, and Mr. Thomson put a hand on her arm. "Do not go, Mrs. Bexley. He has no way of knowing for certain that someone is out here."

She shook her head. "He heard the horses. If I do not reveal myself, he will harm my boys. If he sees one of *you*"—she gestured to the other men crouched in the forest—"he will harm my boys. At the very least, he ought to expect that their mother will wish to come. It will not be a surprise."

"I know that someone is hiding in the forest!" Reddington called. "Reveal yourself now, or I will begin firing my weapons."

"Thank you." Charlotte smiled sadly at Thomson and the others before she turned on her heel and strode determinedly through the copse of trees.

The moment she stepped into the clearing, her gaze and heart were drawn toward her sons. Tears rolled down Quintin's red cheeks, and Maximus sobbed. His heart-wrenching cry of "*Mama!*" was utter agony.

Hugh and Hydra looked appalled to see her, but she cared not. All that concerned her were her sons.

Then, the skies opened up. Rain fell in sheets from the sky, swiftly drenching them all.

"I said *no one else*, Haddington!" Reddington shouted. "Now you've broken that vow twice over."

Charlotte stepped toward the blackguard. "I forced his hand, your lordship. I insisted on being able to see my sons."

The man's face was almost purple in his fury. He aimed his pistol at her and cocked it.

"Mama!" Maximus cried again, his voice thick with tears.

Charlotte's heart constricted, and her throat threatened to close up. "It will be well, my darlings. I promise."

"Enough!" Reddington spat. "Today your sons will witness your death, Mrs. Bexley."

"The pistol will not shoot," Hugh drawled.

Reddington sneered. "Shall we find out?"

"Your shot is wet, and you know it. If it does not fire, you will lose your edge and we'll rush you."

With his other hand, Reddington reached into his waistcoat pocket and withdrew a dagger. Without hesitation, he flipped it in his hand, and threw.

Hugh's shout of "*No!*" reached her just as a shove came from behind, pushing her sideways. A solid *thunk* echoed in her ears as she fell to the ground. Sharp pain rippled up her arm and through her skull when she landed, causing her to cry out. Her eyelids abruptly felt heavy, the weight of her pain and fear for her sons suddenly too much.

* * *

"Charlotte!" Hugh roared. His pulse was erratic as horror rippled through him.

He started at a run toward Charlotte and Thomson, but Maximus' and Quintin's cries stopped him cold in his tracks.

"Move another inch, and I'll throw another," Reddington threatened, aiming this time at Charlotte's sons. "I ought to have known that you would bring more filthy spies to our meeting."

Hugh looked into Quin's terrified gaze and gave his best impression of a reassuring smile. "Your mother is fine, Quin," he called to the boy.

He scowled at Reddington. "You've no ballocks to face a grown man, Reddington? You have to threaten harm to little boys?"

The bastard's face grew ruddy with anger once more. "You'll not speak to me that way!" His chin jutted mutinously. "If you lot won't see reason, I shall have to do more to convince you that I mean what I say."

"Mr. Hugh?" Quin's soft, fearful voice cut Hugh directly through the heart.

"We're not giving up, boys," Hugh assured them. "I will make certain that you are retuned to your mother."

"I believe I'll keep these boys with me until I have precisely what I desire," Reddington mused. "And not a moment sooner. If I see you following…" Reddington left the remainder of his threat unsaid, then gestured toward one of his men. "Take a horse and ride ahead. Prepare for our departure."

The man did as he was bade, taking Percy while Reddington continued to walk the boys slowly backward. Hugh watched with hatred and concern as the cur tossed the boys inside the carriage then shoved his way onto the perch beside his other brute and took over the reins. With one last look over his shoulder, they rolled the carriage into motion and disappeared down the narrow drive, Quin's and Max's cries for help following in their wake.

A flurry of activity erupted the moment the carriage was out of sight. His heart all but stopped, Hugh dashed toward Charlotte, sliding to the muddy ground at her side. Hydra ran toward Thomson, and the other men came out of hiding.

"Charlotte?" Hugh cursed soundly as he pulled The Angel onto his lap. He wiped at the mud that stained her cheek, the shower of rain helping to clear it away.

His worried gaze slid over Thomson. The others surrounded him, but through the throng, Hugh could still see the dagger protruding from Thomson's chest. Blood covered him, and the man coughed. *Damnation*. He needed a doctor immediately.

"Hugh?" Charlotte's sweet voice rang in his ears.

He looked down into her confused light-blue eyes, and smiled. "Thank goodness you're awake," he breathed.

The rain washed the mud away, leaving only her freckles in stark relief against her pallid skin.

"My boys?"

His smile slipped, and guilt roiled in his stomach. "Reddington still has them."

She struggled to rise, and Hugh attempted to help, but she brushed his hand aside. Keeping her face turned away, she stood. The line of her shoulders told him that she was not only in pain from her fall, but furious. He wanted to pull her into his arms and tell her that he was sorry, for Lord knew he'd intended this rendezvous to conclude far differently.

As much as he wished to comfort Mrs. Bexley, there was an injured man to aid. Hugh stood, and joined the other men.

Poor Thomson's eyes were wide and fearful. Hydra held out his hands as a shelter for the man's face.

"I will ride with him back to Brampton," McCully announced.

Hugh shook his head. "He will not survive such a distance."

"He could stay at my home," Charlotte said softly. The men turned to look at her. "I've not a guest bedroom, but he is welcome to take my bed."

Despite the circumstance, Hugh's chest warmed at her offer. She'd done much the same for him in his time of need.

"There is a woman there named Mrs. Laurie," she continued. "Simply tell her that I've given you leave to reside there while I search for my boys."

"I thank you, Mrs. Bexley," Hydra replied. "Brown, ride to Brampton and retrieve Dr. Stainton. McCully, ride carefully with Thomson to Mrs. Bexley's estate. Do you know the direction?"

The man shook his head, and Charlotte quickly provided it.

The others retrieved their mounts from within the copse of trees and returned to the opening. They helped to lift Thomson and bring him to McCully's gelding. The young man was ashen, his expression contorted with pain and fear.

Soon, they had him mounted in front of McCully, but Hydra stalled them.

"Brown, request the aid of more men, if you will. Tell—"

"Pardon the interruption, sir," Colin interjected. "I've already written to Gabe and Mary. They had a greater distance to ride, but will most likely arrive before any men from Brampton."

Hydra inclined his head. "Noted. McCully, when Gabe and Mary arrive, tell them we've gone to the docks. Ride on!"

The men rode off, leaving the four of them behind.

"You're bleeding, Mrs. Bexley," Hydra noted, gesturing to her arm.

Hugh's gaze swung her way, an unsettling ache in his chest. Blood did indeed seep from the wound on her arm, further reddening the browning stain on her green dress.

Charlotte nodded. "I believe I've popped some stitches. I shall be fine."

Hydra eyed her questioningly. "Are you able to ride?"

"I am. And I confess to be rather anxious to leave."

"Mount up!"

Hugh strode toward Charlotte, ready to aid her onto her mare, but her words stopped him.

"Mr. Hydra, would you be so good as to help me onto my horse?"

Hydra nodded. "Of course." He slid an arched sideways glance at Hugh as he strode toward The Angel.

Gritting his teeth against the bewildering anger boiling beneath his skin, Hugh turned and mounted Thomson's gelding.

Hydra swung himself up on his stallion.

"Where is Percy?" The Angel asked.

"One of Reddington's brutes took him," Hugh grunted.

Her lips thinned, but she remained silent. The ride there, the rain, and the mud had taken its toll on her attire and hair, but even with her sopping brown locks half falling and clinging to her neck, she looked breathtaking.

Charlotte walked her mare toward Hugh, Colin, and Hydra. "How do we know that Lord Reddington is taking my boys to the docks?"

"He spoke of preparing for departure," Colin replied. "And, truthfully, it is the only logical option for him if he wishes to avoid the noose."

Worry for the boys, for Charlotte, and for their broken rapport threatened to consume Hugh. Instead of letting it, he channelled that fear into focus and determination.

"Let's ride," Hydra called, urging his stallion into a gallop.

Chapter 19

Hours passed like days as they rode, though Charlotte could credit that to her aching head and the constant, ghastly worry about her sons. Charlotte knew not what time it was, but judging by the gnawing pain in her stomach, she suspected it was nearing the hour of luncheon. The sun was high in the sky, and the clouds had begun to disperse. Her clothing was still damp beneath the layers, but the sun and wind had begun to dry her.

They'd made several stops on the way to London to water, feed, and rest the horses. She'd also taken the opportunity, during their first respite, to seek aid in re-stitching and re-bandaging her wound. It throbbed in time to the beat of her heart, but she scarcely paid it any mind. She was in London to find her sons.

Their mounts' hooves *clip-clopped* over the cobblestoned streets on the outskirts of town as they walked toward the docks. The streets were crowded with carriages, horses, and people bustling about.

"Was his carriage crested?" Mr. Colin Greene asked.

Hugh nodded. "It was. There is a gilt eagle on a shield, with two swords crossed beneath."

"I imagine we won't find the carriage," Hydra mused. "He's probably hidden it in a close or housed it in a stable. It would take far too long for us to find it. Our best option would be to start inquiring about ships bound for the Americas that are leaving port in the next eight-and-forty hours."

"Agreed," Hugh muttered.

Charlotte marvelled at the minds of these men. While evidently unable to comprehend and accept a superior plan—*hers*—their actions were in perfect harmony, and they were able to understand and predict the inner thoughts and motivation of a monster.

A nearby carriage horse whinnied, and the driver shouted to a man carrying a crate of apples toward the docks.

Greene cleared his throat. "If Reddington aimed to board a ship, would he not have sought help?"

"Most definitely." Hydra nodded toward a tie post. "Come, let us inquire in the pubs."

The four of them dismounted and tied off their horses' reins. Charlotte's legs nearly buckled when she landed. Her body ached from the hours of riding, and was bruised from her fall. Her pain notwithstanding, Charlotte was eager to continue on.

They crossed the busy street and entered a tavern. Mr. Greene led the way around the mostly empty tables toward the bartender. Charlotte eyed the few patrons, but didn't see any of Reddington's "brutes," as Hugh had called them.

"Pardon me, sir, but have you happened to see a dandified gentleman with blond hair and green eyes enter?" Mr. Greene asked. "He would very likely be accompanied by two tall, broad men and two young boys."

The bartender shook his head, his shaggy mane of grey hair rubbing against his shoulders. "I ain't seen none that look like tha'."

Hugh leaned forward, resting his forearms on the bar. "Do you happen to know if there are any ships setting sail for the Americas in the next two days?" He slid some coins across the bar's surface, and the bartender's eyes widened with greed.

"Aye, there are three." The man pocketed the coins, then picked up a wet cloth and wiped his hands. "I hear tell there's 'un leavin' at one-o'-th'-clock tomorrow, an' two leavin' later in th' afternoon."

"Thank you very much, sir." Hugh tossed the man another two coins, nodding.

Charlotte's pulse sped. *Three ships.* Her sons could be headed for any of them. "What time is it?"

Hydra withdrew and flipped open his pocket watch as they strode toward the tavern's door. "Half of one."

The door creaked, and Charlotte squinted into the sun as they opened it.

"We have some time before the ships are set to sail," Hugh said in an undertone as they strode down the footway. "What do you suppose is the likelihood that Reddington will have boarded the boys this early?"

Mr. Greene opened his mouth to reply, but before he could respond, a sharp exclamation sounded behind her.

"Charlotte?" A man gasped. "*Charlotte?*"

She turned to see a tall, imposing man standing ten paces behind her. He wore a charcoal coat and breeches, a grey embroidered waistcoat, starched white shirt and cravat, and shining black Hessians. The man's ornamentation was minimal: a blood-red ruby was pinned to his neck cloth, which matched the ruby on his little finger. His hair was grey beneath his tall black hat and curling at his ears, and his shoulders were broad and strong, though his stomach had begun to grow soft with age. There were the beginnings of wrinkles around his eyes and mouth, and the glittering light-blue of his gaze sparkled with recognition.

Charlotte knew him immediately.

He breathed in a ragged gasp, a grimace of emotion on his handsomely aged features as he strode quickly toward her.

Frozen with uncertainty and the shock of recognition, Charlotte stood stiff while the man crushed her in a forward embrace. Her arm screamed in pain, but she pushed it from her mind, instead taking in the moment. The seconds rushed by as he pressed his cheek to her mud-crusted hair.

As much as she attempted to hold them back, the embrace merely urged her feelings to the fore. She blinked at the hot sting of tears, but several spilled over her eyelids.

The man released her, and Hugh and his fellows bent in appropriate bows.

She wiped at her damp cheeks. "Mr. Haddington, Mr. Greene, and Sir Bradley, this is—"

"Thank you, Mrs. Bexley. We know who he is." Hydra smiled at the man over Charlotte's shoulder. "The Duke of Norshire. A pleasure to see you again, Your Grace."

"The pleasure is all mine, I assure you." The duke beamed. "You've returned my daughter to me!"

* * *

Hugh's stomach plummeted. "*You're* Lady Charlotte Lucille Morris?"

"I was." The Angel's lips thinned. "Until I married and was disowned."

The duke sputtered. "You were never *disowned*, Charlotte. That bastard of a man, Mr. Bexley, poisoned your mind; he convinced you of that nonsense when it was far from the truth. Your mother and I wanted—hoped for—an advantageous marriage for you, but we would have accepted whatever decision you made. Then you disappeared with the man, and we had no way to know where you went."

"How could you not have known?" Charlotte's eyes were wide with emotion. "We lived in the home that my husband had bought from his aunt—"

His Grace shook his head. "Not his aunt, pigeon. I've searched from the morning that you left for Gretna until this very day. The cur never had any properties bequeathed to him or sold by any family member."

Charlotte stood mute. An array of emotions swept across The Angel's features, from disbelief and shock to resolution and acceptance. Hugh wished that he could offer her some comfort, but it was not his place.

Good God, he'd tupped a duke's daughter. What in the bloody hell had he done? She deserved satins and silks, the opera, jewels, and a lord of the realm, not a lowly orphan who had been plucked from the streets and raised a spy.

Shame engulfed him.

"Pardon the forwardness of my inquiry," Hydra said, breaking the brief silence, "but have you found Lady Laura?"

The duke's blue eyes—*Charlotte's* blue eyes, *damn it*—turned sad. "I'm afraid not. That is what I'm doing here, you see. There are ships setting sail, and I'd hoped to have a man on each, prepared to bring her home if they found her."

Hugh had read about the incident in the paper yesterday morning. Someone had stolen into The Duke's home in the middle of the night and taken Lady Laura Morris from her bed. The note left on her pillow had hinted at a pirate with a personal vendetta against His Grace.

"I'm so sorry, Your Grace," Hugh replied.

The duke regally nodded in thanks. "I miss her and worry for her dreadfully, but…now I have at least *one* of my daughters returned to me." He smiled sadly. "I shan't look the gift horse in the mouth, but I confess I am curious. What brings you to the docks this afternoon?"

Charlotte wiped again at her damp cheeks, and Hugh's chest tightened.

"My sons were taken from me. We followed the kidnapper here, and we're searching for them."

"I have grandsons," His Grace breathed. "What of Mr. Bexley? Is he not here to search, as well?"

She shook her head. "My husband died nearly five years ago."

The duke's lips thinned. "It would appear that you and I have much to discuss. If you would let me, I would be honoured to help find my grandsons." His piercing blue gaze lifted to Hugh, Hydra, and Colin. "What can I do?"

"I must forewarn you, Your Grace, that the kidnapper is a lord of the realm…" Hugh described Reddington and his brutes as quickly and concisely as possible.

"We must divide ourselves into three groups and search the frigates simultaneously." Hydra pointed at Colin. "You—"

"Might I be paired with you, Sir Bradley?" Charlotte asked, her sweet voice cutting Hugh to the quick.

"Of course." Hydra narrowed his gaze at Hugh, but the meaning behind the look was lost on him.

Hugh wanted to protest, to express his desire to be paired with Charlotte. But he had no claim on her, and she very clearly had no wish to spend time in his company.

A foreign quivering rippled through his abdomen, and he suppressed a snarl of distaste.

"In my inquiries, I've learned that the frigate set to disembark at one-of-the-clock tomorrow sits in the River Thames to the west of the main docks," His Grace said. "I will fetch two armed footmen and search it under the pretence of inspecting the ship's readiness for my potential cargo."

Hugh nodded. "We will take the ship to the east of the main docks."

"That leaves the south for us," Hydra rumbled. "Before you cross the water, add crates or barrels to your boat to draw the attention away from you. If you appear to be a crewman preparing to depart, you might divert eyes. If you find Reddington, whistle thrice sharply; the sound should carry on the water. Most importantly…be careful."

Charlotte avoided eye contact as she turned to follow Hydra, and Hugh's heart twisted painfully.

He nodded at Colin, and the two set out toward the docks.

The moment they were out of earshot, Colin muttered, "Is there some ill will between you and Mrs. Bexley?" He lowered his voice a fraction. "Perhaps a lovers' quarrel?"

Hugh cursed. "Bloody hell, Colin."

"Ah." His friend nodded. "I am correct. What did you do?"

"What makes you so certain that I 'did' something?" He had done, of course, but he didn't want Colin to know that.

"Gabriel asked the same thing about his treatment of Mary." Colin raised an eyebrow at Hugh. "And now they're to be wed."

Hugh shook his head. "It isn't like that."

"No?"

They passed a fishmonger selling his wares, and the scent of fish and the reeking water of the Thames assailed his senses. Hugh wheezed a rough cough. Their footfalls sounded hollow on the dock's planks as they made their way to the end.

"No. It isn't," Hugh affirmed, though he wasn't so certain of it himself. As much as he hated to admit it, he'd not thought that far ahead. He knew that he wanted her, that he wished to spend more time in her company, but as for a future… "No," he reiterated. "She's a duke's daughter, for God's sake."

Reaching the end of the dock, they approached a man near to a rowing boat. "Might you be the owner of this rowing boat?" Hugh asked.

"Yessir." The man smiled to reveal blackened teeth. "Wanna borrow it?"

"Indeed we do." Colin withdrew his purse. "Do you happen to know which of the frigates to the east of this dock are bound for the Americas on the morrow?"

"That 'un there." The man pointed to a frigate sitting low in the water—apparently heavy with cargo—then accepted his coin from Colin.

With a nod of thanks, they settled in the boat already containing two crates, and began to row. Hugh's healing shoulder injury ached with each movement, but he ground his teeth and pushed through it. He could use a little pain to distract him.

From Charlotte—or, rather, Lady Charlotte Lucille Morris.

How could he have lost control of their situation? Hugh hated that she and the boys had been put into such danger. He oughtn't have let her nurse him so long; as soon as he had been able to stand, he should have borrowed a mount or a wagon and journeyed to Brampton. He ought to have told her the truth from the start.

"Just because she's a duke's daughter does not mean that you cannot have her." Colin's voice cut into his inner rebuke.

Hugh's jaw jumped. "Of course it does. She deserves a man of rank."

"She married Mr. Bexley, did she not?"

"Yes, and see where that got her."

Colin frowned at him. "You are not Mr. Bexley. And you cannot live your life comparing yourself or your circumstance to others; it will make you miserable and bloody intolerable."

Pulling harder on the oars in anger, Hugh grunted. "Enough. My life isn't ideal at the moment, Colin, or hadn't you noticed?" He notched his chin to the side and glanced around at the River Thames. "Tell me, how did you become so knowledgeable about life?" he asked, sarcasm dripping from his voice.

"Merely reporting my observations, Hugh." Colin's expression shuttered, but he replied honestly, "I've nothing particularly eventful in my life at present. I broke things off with my mistress—"

"Nora?"

Colin nodded. "We began to lose interest in each other, and I'm certain that she's taken on other lovers. Now, it's been over a month since I've lain with a woman."

"Poor Colin."

"I know it." His friend grinned, his eyes knowing.

They drew closer to the frigate, their boat moving at a steady pace. A sweat had broken out over Hugh's forehead and dripped down his back. It had been far too long since he'd done genuine labour, and with the weight that he'd lost during his imprisonment, he fought yet harder to do even menial tasks.

"How is your sister?" Hugh ground out, eager to prevent his thoughts from wandering to Charlotte again.

Colin's lips thinned grimly. "Isobel is not well, I'm afraid. Another bout of melancholy. How fares Philip? Have you informed him of your—"

"I haven't, no. I intend to, however, once this is over."

They slipped into silence as they rowed nearer the frigate, and, despite his efforts, Hugh's thoughts were once more drawn to *Lady Charlotte Morris*, and Colin's words. The thought of being with her was far too tempting, but now that she'd been reunited with her family, would she not wish to wed a man of wealth and rank?

"You would make each other happy, Hugh." Colin cut into his thoughts once more. "Best make amends for whatever wrong you did to her, and live your life to the fullest."

Crack! Hugh's gut jumped, and his senses grew instantly alert as a shot hit the water beside their boat.

"Looks like we have the correct ship!" Colin laughed, pulling harder on the oars.

Hugh scrunched his lips and let out a shrill whistle, just as another *crack* rent the air.

Chapter 20

Charlotte grimaced as she pulled the oars through the water. Her arm pained her something fierce, but, if it meant finding her sons, she would put herself through any amount of discomfort.

"You needn't row, Mrs. Bexley," Hydra said softly. "We are nearing the frigate, and I can take us the remainder of the way."

"It is quite all right. I am eager to retrieve my sons, and I fear that I wouldn't know what to do with my nervous energy if I just sat and waited."

His eyes crinkled in the corners. "You sound much like my wife."

"She must be lovely." Charlotte smiled at him.

"Indeed, Bridget is the best woman I've ever known. I'm a very lucky man." Hydra's eyes warmed at the thought of his wife, and Charlotte felt a twinge of envy.

Would that she could have a love such as his. What sort of a life could she have, however, if she dared not trust men?

"If you and your wife found yourselves in a perilous circumstance, would you attempt to shield her from danger by withholding the truth?"

He eyed her shrewdly for a moment before he laughed. "If I did not know better of it, I would say that you've spoken directly to Bridget." He chuckled again before he gazed at her openly. "*You* know that I work in the Secret Service, but I hid that fact from Bridget for above two years after my return from war. I treated her abhorrently in an attempt to distance myself from her…to protect her from danger. Hell, even after the threat to her life, I told falsehoods and planned an elaborate scheme in my foolish effort to keep her safe."

He raised an eyebrow at her. "None among my trained men and women live a life of full truth. We learn to lie as easily as we breathe air, and we do everything in our power to protect the innocent."

Charlotte's pulse sped as the man spoke.

"Are you well?" Hydra asked softly.

She smiled sadly at him. "No. But I believe I will be."

"Hugh is a good man," Hydra called down to her. "I've known him for many years, and—"

Crack!

Hydra cursed and his gaze swung to the left. "Gunfire!" he shouted.

A shrill whistle sounded, though it was faint to her ears, and terror iced through her veins, her heart slamming in her chest as the implications hit.

Crack!

* * *

"Holy hell," Hugh cursed as he struggled up the rope ladder.

It was a race for survival as the brutes attempted to cut through the thick rope at the top.

Hugh's body screamed in protest at every movement. He'd not slept the previous evening, having ridden through the night, and it was beginning to take its toll.

The brutes swung blades at him as he neared the top. One knife grazed his forearm, cutting easily through the material of his sleeve. With a roar of pain, Hugh reached high, gripped the man's cravat, and pulled. The brute cried out in alarm as he lost his balance and toppled over the railing, falling to the water below with a *splash.*

"Blimey," Colin muttered below Hugh on the ladder. "Well done."

The other brute shuffled away in fear, and Hugh clambered over the frigate's rail. Colin followed closely behind him, and immediately advanced on Reddington's man. His breath coming quickly, Hugh swung his gaze around the upper deck.

"Where the devil *is* everyone?" Hugh wondered aloud. Several crewmen went about their duties; their curious stares swung his way, but none appeared to be a threat.

"Don't bloody care," Colin muttered as he set his sights on Reddington's other man. "Reddington and Mrs. Bexley's sons must be belowdecks," he called to Hugh as he unsheathed his dagger and lunged at the brute. "Go on, Hugh! I have him."

Needing no further provocation, Hugh withdrew his pistol and ran toward the forehatch, his injuries and aches notwithstanding. Hastening down the stairs, he reached the main hatchway. He glanced about then strode carefully forward, passing into the gunroom. Men surrounded him, but none came forward.

"Have you seen a man with two small boys come through here?" he asked, a note of desperation seeping into his voice.

Several of the men shook their heads, and Hugh descended onto the mess deck. Crewmen carried buckets of water and other items around, but they paid him no mind. He made his way toward the officers' cabins and opened each door, peering carefully inside before moving on to the next.

Finally, he descended onto the orlop, his fear and sheer fucking panic making his lungs labour and fingers tremble. *Sodding hell*, but he'd never experienced such feelings, most particularly while on assignment. What if this were a ruse? What if Reddington had sent his men to this ship, but the boys were somewhere else?

He tried to listen past his speeding pulse and rapid breathing, but all he could hear were the heavy footfalls of the crewmen, the creaking of wood, and the faint sounds of sloshing water as the ship gently rocked.

* * *

A bead of perspiration trickled between Charlotte's breasts as she rowed. They'd covered half the distance to the frigate that Mr. Greene and Hugh had boarded, but the minutes seemed to be crawling by.

She pushed hard on the oars, gazing up at the large ship. The masts reached high to the bright sky, the sails were furled, and the rigging looked like spiders' webs dotted with men. There was movement on the main deck, but at that distance, she could not see who it was.

A growl escaped her.

Sir Bradley—Hydra—turned to look over his shoulder, and cursed. The worry on his face mirrored what she felt, and she experienced a moment of commonality. He was a father who would worry over the safety of his children, as well.

"Thank you," she said breathlessly.

Hydra caught her gaze. "You're welcome. Let's fetch your sons."

Hugh made his way to the next deck and searched through the main hold, his body in utter turmoil. There were barrels and crates filled with goods, but no children hidden behind them. He thought to call out, but he didn't wish to alert Reddington to his presence, if it wasn't already known.

Hell, but he'd made a promise to see those boys returned to their mother, and he couldn't let them down. Couldn't let *Charlotte* down.

There were other closed doors at the end of the main hold, and Hugh strode purposefully toward them. He picked the one to his left, pressed the latch with trembling fingers, and swung the door inward.

He squinted into the darkness as he stepped over the threshold. Then, he saw them.

"Quintin! Maximus!" he uttered in a harsh whisper, his heart pounding. Sheer bloody relief washed over him, and, to his amazement, the prickle of tears sprang to his eyes.

The boys' eyes were wide and fearful, their mouths covered by filthy cloth and their wrists and ankles tied with rough rope. The anger already burning through Hugh bubbled hotter as he noted the state of them. Their clothes were tattered, and their skin was filthy and covered in scratches.

Guilt and fear lingered with his anger; his entire body rocked with the force of it. He ought to have listened to Charlotte's suggestions, ought to have considered her ideas, and, *hell*, he ought to have told her the truth from the start; maybe they could have avoided all of this.

Hugh tugged at the fabric covering the boys' mouths. "I'm here to return you to your mother," he whispered. "Are you well?"

Tears flooded Maximus' eyes, and Hugh fought his own, swallowing hard against the lump forming in his throat.

Quintin nodded. "We just want to go home."

"I will bring you there as soon as poss—"

Something moved beneath Maximus' waistcoat, and Hugh blinked.

"That's Jack," Maximus whispered, his voice wavering. "He's hungry and wants to run around."

Hugh looked inquisitively at Quintin.

"Jack is a kitten," Quin answered the unspoken question.

With a nod, Hugh put his pistol on the floor at his feet and set to untying the knots. He began with Quin's ankles, quickly freeing them, and then moved on to Max's.

Hugh despised seeing The Angel's sons this way. He'd never seen them anything but vibrant and playful. It crushed him.

The tie for Max's ankles slipped free, and Hugh reached for the boy's wrists.

"Put your hands in the air, and turn around," came a sophisticated drawl from the doorway behind him, followed by the *click* of a pistol being cocked.

Hugh silently cursed and slowly stood, wishing that he hadn't abandoned his weapon on the ground. His arms up and palms facing forward, he turned to see Reddington blocking the dim light from beyond the door.

"Say goodbye to the blighters, Haddington."

The blackguard's hand began to tighten, and Hugh reacted instinctively. Taking three steps at a run, Hugh gripped Reddington's pistol-wielding wrist, and lifted.

Bang!

* * *

Charlotte stretched as she strained to get a better look at the men on deck. The two men threw punches, then locked arms and propelled themselves against the railing. Neither of them were Hugh.

The sweat at her temples gathered and slid down her hairline to her jaw as she rowed. *So close!* They were only a few yards away from the rope ladder.

A muted *bang* came from within the frigate, and Charlotte's heart stalled. "Was that—?"

Hydra cursed under his breath, his sweat-misted lips pulled in a thin line. "I'm afraid that it was."

Horrid images flashed through her mind. Were her sons well? Was *Hugh?* She didn't know what she would do with herself if—

Thunk. The rowing boat bumped against the side of the frigate, and she was shaken from her dark thoughts.

* * *

Hugh's ears rang with a high-pitched hum as he tackled Reddington to the ground. The bastard's spent pistol bounced off the coarse wooden floor and slid away, and, without preamble, Hugh clambered atop him and struck the man's face with his fist. One. Two. Three. Four strikes before Reddington's eyes slid closed and his arms went limp.

With a grimace of distaste, Hugh wiped his bloodied knuckles on Reddington's coat, then returned his attention to the boys.

"Are either of you hurt?" he asked over his shoulder, his throat thick with worry.

Both boys shook their heads, their eyes wide with fright.

"Good." He notched his chin toward them. "Would you be so good as to toss that rope to me, please?"

With a short nod, Quin selected one of the ropes that had tied the boys' ankles, and tossed it with both hands toward Hugh. Hugh gave a nod of thanks, then turned to restrain Reddington.

The bit of rope was too small for the grown man's wrists, but it would do well enough until Hydra and the others made their way to the frigate.

That done, he knelt before the boys and resumed the untying of their restraints.

With the boys freed, and Hugh's pistol returned to the leather holster hidden in his coat, Hugh helped them to their feet. They were silent as they moved, hurrying past their captor and into the frigate's hold.

Curious gazes followed them through the ship, but Hugh paid the inept crewmen no mind. How could they not have known that two little boys were just recently brought onto the ship?

Before they reached the stairs leading to the fore hatch, Hugh stopped Quin and Max with a subtle gesture of his hand and put his index finger to his lips. "I must see if the way is clear," he whispered. He was confident that Colin could best the brute, but one never did know with complete certainty which party would win in combat.

Hugh pressed the latch and lifted the angled door, swinging it wide, then cautiously peered through.

Colin knelt upon the brute, his knee digging into the large man's back as he tied a bloodied cravat around the man's wrists. With a grand smile of triumph on his lips, Colin swung his gaze to Hugh. "The bugger is enormous, but I bested him!" With one last nudge to the unconscious man, Colin stood. "Where are Mrs. Bexley's sons?"

Relief and mirth tugged Hugh's lips into a smile, and he turned to usher the boys onto the main deck. They squinted into the sunlight as they emerged, and Hugh's heart tugged.

Hydra topped the rope ladder and swung himself over the rail, and Charlotte appeared a moment later. Hugh's heart leapt at the sight of her.

"*Maximus*!" she cried in relief. "*Quintin*!"

"*Mama*!" The boys ran to her as she knelt on the main deck, and she enveloped them in a crushing hug, sudden tears streaming down her cheeks.

"Wait!" Maximus protested, pulling away to withdraw a small orange kitten from his waistcoat. He extended his arm outward, handing the ball of fur to Hydra. "Here, mister. Please hold Jack."

"Of course," Hydra muttered, bemused, accepting the little beastie.

Something in Hugh's chest ached at the sight of The Angel weeping over her sons' return. She squeezed them tightly, pressing kisses to their matted hair and dirt-streaked faces. Unbidden, Hugh's throat thickened, and a slight sting began behind his eyes.

He cleared his throat with a harsh cough. "Sir." He stepped a pace toward Hydra. "Reddington remains below deck. I've knocked him unconscious, but—"

"*Hugh*!" Hydra exclaimed.

Bang!

Chapter 21

Charlotte's heart slammed in her chest as Hugh wavered, then crumpled limply to the ground. Mr. Greene attempted to wrest the pistol from Reddington's hand, but had failed to prevent the hit.

Her boys hugged her tighter, and she hushed them reassuringly. "Mama has you. All will be well." But she wasn't certain of that fact at all.

Mr. Greene and Sir Bradley moved so quickly that Charlotte had scarcely a moment to realize what was happening. In a series of mystifying movements, the men had Lord Reddington's nose bloodied and pressed against the main deck.

"Use mine." Sir Bradley tugged with one hand at the knot of his cravat, easily untying it before slipping it from around his neck and handing it to Greene. Charlotte noted with astonishment that Hydra still held her sons' kitten in the palm of his left hand.

The threat defused, Charlotte wiped at her cheeks and whispered to her sons, "Stay here, boys."

They nodded, holding hands as she turned. There were but mere steps between her and Hugh, but Charlotte ran to him, nonetheless. A sob caught in her throat as she knelt beside him. He lay face down on the wooden planks, a small pool of blood slowly growing beneath his abdomen.

Sir Bradley cursed, joining her at Hugh's side. "He requires medical attention."

"I'll not be put in a noose!" Reddington shouted as he fought against Mr. Greene's hold.

Ignoring the blackguard's curses and incoherent babbling, Charlotte leaned close to Hugh's face. She gently brushed locks of his dark blond, wavy hair from his forehead and listened for his breathing. A gentle gust of air escaped his nose, and relief flooded her. *He is alive.* It would be a fight for him to remain that way, but she'd damned well do her best.

The memory of him broken, beaten, and smelling of refuse on the floor of the shack on Reddington's land flashed through her mind, and her chest tightened. The man had been through so much physical abuse in the past months, she was astonished that his body had withstood it all.

She bent closer, continuing to brush his forelocks from his face. "Hugh," she urged.

Lord, but it hurt her heart to see him thusly.

"You'll not put me on trial! I'll not be put into gaol!" Reddington shouted, twisting and fighting as Sir Bradley and Mr. Greene lifted him to his feet.

Their heavy footsteps rumbled the main deck's planks as they strode past, and a low groan emanated from Hugh, drawing everyone's attention.

Charlotte's breath hitched. "Hugh?"

"I'll not be taken!" Reddington took advantage of their distraction to wrest himself away, and he ran toward her boys.

"Reddington, stop!" Hydra called.

Charlotte stood, her pulse racing and her stomach dropping. "Boys! Look out!"

Reddington leapt at her sons, taking them over the ship's railing with him, the boys' shrieks fading as they fell.

"*No!*" Charlotte screamed as she ran, the splash of the water muffled behind the heartbeat thudding in her ears.

She slammed into the railing, looking over its edge. "Quin! Max!" Had they hit the two rowing boats on the way down?

Without a moment's hesitation, Charlotte lifted herself over the rail and descended the rope ladder, her ever-present sense of terror riding her mercilessly. She'd only just gotten them back—she couldn't lose them now!

* * *

Hugh blinked, his eyes focusing on the sun-bleached main deck of the frigate. *What the devil?* He lifted his head, and groaned at the shooting pain in his ribs.

A steady ringing filled his ears, but behind it he heard sharp screams and the thudding of footsteps. His breathing was shallow and quick, the stab in his ribs preventing him from taking a deep breath.

He struggled to rise and to make sense of what was happening around him. He squinted at the retreating figures. Charlotte was first, then Hydra and Colin. They looked over the edge of the rail, shouted something, and then Charlotte led the descent.

Giving his head a quick, painful shake, Hugh finally stood. Agony shot through his side and he looked down. Blood soaked his front.

"Holy hell," he slurred, putting a hand to his side.

Cringing at the pain, he felt an entry and exit wound along his ribs. The wound was shallow, but the shot must have ricocheted off his rib, very likely breaking it. He'd lost a great deal of blood.

He looked around the deck; the only remaining evidence of their presence was the unconscious brute lying ten paces away from him and the stain of Hugh's blood on the deck. His gaze swung to the rope ladder, where Colin's head was disappearing, and he staggered toward it.

Blinking away the spots in his vision, Hugh looked down to the water as he reached the railing. Charlotte, Hydra, and Colin raced down the rope ladder, swaying with their efforts, and in the water… Hugh cursed foully under his breath. In the water, the boys were sputtering and trying to stay afloat as the Thames lapped at their frightened faces.

Hugh's heart clenched. They were too far from the boats, the river's current drawing them further away. They'd not make it.

Instinct driving him, Hugh removed his coat, gritting his teeth at the anguish caused by both his ribs and the worry in his mind, and dove over the railing into the water below. The chill of the water was a shock to his system, urging him to gasp as he broke the surface.

"Mr. Hugh!" Maximus cried out, his arms flapping in the water nearby.

Hugh's lip quivered with the cold—or perhaps he was going into shock? "Grab on to me, boys. That's it, hands on my shoulders."

He could scarcely breathe, but he pushed past the pain, focusing on his main goal of bringing the boys to the boats. Being an experienced swimmer meant very little when one struggled against the River Thames with a likely broken rib, but try, Hugh did.

Charlotte and Hydra reached the first boat, and began to row toward them.

"Here they come, b-boys." Hugh's voice sounded weak, even to his own ears.

Exhaustion overcame him, and he fought to keep his feet kicking. *Just get the boys on the boat*, his mind urged.

The boat arrived, and the boys called for their mother. Hugh reached to his shoulder and pulled Maximus forward through the water. Gripping the boy beneath his arms and along his ribs, Hugh lifted him toward Hydra's waiting hands. The action lowered Hugh's head below the water's surface and forced Quin to let go of his shoulder.

Hugh sputtered as he found the air once more, and he reached to help Quintin into Hydra's arms. Agony screamed through Hugh's body. *The boys are safe. You can rest now.*

His eyes slid closed as a feeling of liberation filled him. He'd righted his wrongs with both the boys and Charlotte. They could be content once more.

Just because she's a duke's daughter does not mean that you cannot have her. Colin's words repeated in Hugh's mind. *You would make each other happy, Hugh…live your life to the fullest.*

There was a muted shout, and Hugh realized that he'd sunk beneath the water. Great sadness swept over him. *I'll never be able to tell Charlotte that I love her.*

He sank deeper, and the awareness dawned. *Good God!* His eyes popped open in the water. *I love Charlotte!*

* * *

"Oh, my boys!" Charlotte extended her other arm to encompass Quintin as he was brought upon the boat.

Hydra looked over at Mr. Greene, who rowed the other boat. "The boys are safe!"

"As is their feline," Greene called back, gesturing to the meowing mass in his waistcoat.

Charlotte grinned, then pressed kisses to her sons' sopping hair. "Are you both well? Were you hurt falling to the water?"

The boys mumbled incoherently into the front of her soiled frock, shivering and coughing. She held them closer, then turned her gaze back to the water. And her heart froze as she scanned its surface.

"Where is Hugh?"

Hydra cursed.

"*Hugh*!" she called. The now-familiar terror chilled her heart once more. "Stay here with Sir Bradley, boys." Charlotte set her sons away from her and stood, rocking the small boat with her movement.

"Mrs. Bexley—" Hydra began.

"Where is he?" she called back to Sir Bradley. "Do you see him?"

She would be damned if she let another man she loved die. The sudden recognition of her feelings was both elating and defeating, for she might never be able to tell him…

"Mama!" Maximus shouted, his voice hoarse. He pointed just beyond her in the water. "There!"

Charlotte's gaze swung around, scanning the water. *There!* She spotted the white of his lawn shirtsleeves floating below the surface, and her heart nigh stopped.

"No! He can't die today. He'll not drown." *Like my husband…* The words were left unsaid, but they screeched through her mind as she leapt into the water.

The shock of the cold took her breath away, but she pushed past it and dove.

With her eyes closed, she couldn't see him through the water, but she kept her arms outstretched, hoping to make contact.

Then, she felt him. Her fingers raked through his waving hair, and she hastily moved her hands to grip his waistcoat and pulled, kicking with all her might.

They broke the water's surface, and she gasped. "I have him!"

She struggled, kicking and panting, to get him to the boat, until hands reached out toward them. Hydra gripped Hugh and pulled him on board. Charlotte held on to the side of the boat, her chest heaving as she awaited assistance. Soon, Sir Bradley turned and aided her into the boat.

Despite there being a seat next to her sons, Charlotte sat on the boat's floor with Hugh. His skin was pale—almost blue—and he was entirely motionless.

She put a hand before his nose, but felt no air. "He's not breathing! How can I get him to breathe?" she asked, helplessness and panic tightening her throat. "What do I do?"

Sir Bradley knelt on the floor, as well. "I've seen someone perform this with success." He glanced at her briefly, then bent forward. Sir Bradley pinched Hugh's nose, pressed down on his jaw, and put his mouth to Hugh's.

Hydra's sharp exhale pushed Hugh's cheeks outward, but Hugh didn't react. Charlotte sat back on her heels, watching anxiously as Sir Bradley repeated the action several times. Nervousness and fear raced through her.

An odd notion occurred to her. Would not pressing on his stomach or chest urge the water out? One did not know until one tried, and at that moment she would have done anything to have him live. She put a hand to his abdomen and one to his chest, and pushed after Sir Bradley had finished blowing. He nodded encouragingly at her, and blew again before Charlotte pushed.

Sir Bradley bent to put his mouth to Hugh's once more when Hugh sputtered.

"Hugh!" Her heart leapt, and she helped him to turn over as he retched, river water splashing over the boat's side.

Relief washed over her. He was by no means healed, but just to have him breathing was most certainly a battle won.

Hugh coughed, and his body shook as he took in deep, quivering gasps. When he was done heaving, Hugh's tremors took over. Charlotte pulled him onto her lap and wrapped her arms around him.

"You will be well, Hugh," she crooned. "We will get you to a surgeon."

Hydra picked up the oars and called over to Mr. Greene. "Return to shore and find the Duke of Norshire. Ask him if we might have use of his carriage. Then ride ahead and summon Dr. Claridge, and have some men return to retrieve Reddington's brute and search for his lordship's body." His jaw clenched. "We're headed to the safe house in town."

Colin nodded and began rowing quickly to shore.

Hugh's bloodshot green eyes cracked open, squinting into the sun as he looked up at her, and Charlotte's heart swelled with emotion.

"My…" he croaked, a faint smile touching his lips. "My Angel has rescued me again."

Chapter 22

Doctor Lord Simon Claridge, the Earl of Merrington, knelt over Hugh, holding an odd, cylindrical stick between his ear and Hugh's chest. He'd been standing thusly for several moments, moving the tube about Hugh's bandaged torso, and the suspense was too much to be borne for Charlotte.

Finally, the doctor stood, returning his implements to his black leather bag and then turning to Hydra and Charlotte. He was a handsome man with pitch-dark hair and piercing blue eyes. He was apparently married to Hydra's sister by marriage. Despite his pleasing form, at the moment, he appeared grim.

"I'm afraid that his condition is poor, indeed," the doctor said. The low, soothing timbre of his voice did nothing to ease the painful ache in her chest. "There is water in his lungs. It was fortunate that you retrieved him from the river, but it is very likely that he will still drown. He is encouraged to cough up the water, but as he has broken two ribs, it will be unquestionably painful, and possibly detrimental to the healing of his bones. I may be required to reset them."

The ache in Charlotte's chest worsened with every word that the doctor uttered.

"Thank you, Simon." Sir Bradley stepped forward and shook the man's hand.

Dr. Claridge nodded. "Of course, Charles. Shall we see to the two boys?"

Momentarily shaken out of her melancholy, Charlotte cleared her throat. "Yes, please, Doctor. They are in the next room."

They moved from the room together, leaving Hugh alone in the bed. Her mind raced as they strode the short walk down the hall. Hydra had given His Grace's coachman the direction of a house in town, which Charlotte surmised was the "safe house" for Hydra's Secret Service spies.

The building was large but ordinary from the outside, while the inside was rather extraordinary. The foyer was grand, with marble floors, white walls, and silver trappings, and the halls were panelled with dark wood and run with burgundy carpets. Charlotte admired the expensive beeswax candles and the immaculate cleanliness, but she wasn't terribly surprised. The home was bustling with activity, and likely had many hands doing regular dusting and polishing.

"Mama!" Maximus bounced on his knees before the hearth, where a low, warm fire was burning.

"How fares Mr. Hugh, Mama?" Quintin asked.

Sudden tears sprang to her eyes, but she blinked them back as she walked further into the room. "He has a great deal of healing to do." She knelt beside the boys, where they were wiggling pieces of string before their little orange kitten, and she gestured toward the doctor. "This is Dr. Claridge. He has come to have a look at you."

* * *

"I'm so glad that you've arrived," Colin said, relief filling him as Gabriel Ashley—Baron Winning—and Mary Wright strode through the door from the back gardens into the kitchens.

Gabriel stood tall and imposing, his brown hair curling over his ears and his blue eyes piercing. He nodded at Colin as he closed the door behind himself. Mary smiled sadly at Colin, her grey eyes glistening as she pulled her bonnet off to reveal her bright auburn hair.

She strode forward and pulled him into her embrace. "We departed as soon as we received your missive."

"We saw Thomson and McCully at Mrs. Bexley's estate," Gabe said in his flowing Scottish accent as he strode forward. "They directed us 'ere. Said they'd be borrowing Mrs. Laurie's carriage and coming te town, as well."

Colin released Mary and shook Gabe's hand. "How did Thomson fare?"

Gabe winced. "He didnae say he was in particular pain, but he didnae have te. McCully did a verra fine job stitching 'im up, though." His mien grew solemn. "How is Hugh?"

"How did you know?" Colin's voice grew thick and his stomach gave an odd flip as he thought of his ailing friend.

Gabe notched his chin toward Colin. "'Tis written upon yer face, my friend."

With a sigh, Colin began. While they spoke, he hung his friends' outerwear on pegs, and they prepared tea trays for the home's inhabitants.

"Have our men found Lord Reddington?" Mary asked, wiping her hands on a cloth.

"No." Colin shook his head. "Not as of yet."

They were silent for a moment as Gabe cut sandwiches into small triangles and put them on plates and Mary poured boiling water into teapots.

"Has Barrows awoken?" Mary's soft inquiry broke their silence.

Barrows, the poor blighter, had been attacked some weeks prior and had yet to regain consciousness from the blow to his head. He slept abovestairs in a guest bedchamber near to Hugh's.

"I'm afraid not," Colin replied. "We've been dripping broth into his mouth to keep him alive, but he's growing frail."

"These are ready." Gabe lifted a tray in his hands. "Is Hydra in his office?"

Colin inclined his head. "I imagine so."

"One of these is for Mrs. Bexley?" Mary asked quietly as Gabe quit the room.

Colin's lips pulled into a mirthless smile. "I will bring a tray to her, if you would be so good as to bring one to her sons."

Mary returned his smile and lifted a tray. "Of course. I love children."

"They will require aid in pouring," he reminded her as she strode out of the kitchens.

Colin lifted the last tray and trod from the room. He'd wanted to have the opportunity to speak with Gabriel about the inheritance of his title, the state of his estate, and many other things, but the current sombre environment of the safe house told him to save such discussions until later.

He reached Mrs. Bexley's bedchamber but found the room empty. Colin ought to have known that she would not be there. Turning from the room, he continued down the hall until he reached Hugh's bedchamber and swept through the opened doorway. He quietly placed the tray on a nearby table and turned toward the bed.

There Mrs. Bexley was, seated in a chair at Hugh's bedside and holding his hand in hers, her waist bent and her head resting on the bed. Despite the dismal circumstance, a genuine smile tugged at Colin's lips. The woman was clearly exhausted, but cared enough for his friend that she remained by his side.

Colin was about to slip from the room, but Hugh's movement stopped him. Striding forward, he watched his friend carefully.

Beads of sweat had formed on Hugh's brow, upper lip, and chest, and his cheeks were flushed, but the rest of his exposed skin was ashen. As he looked on, Hugh began to groan and thrash agitatedly. Colin's heart sank.

Careful not to startle Mrs. Bexley, Colin placed a hand on her shoulder and gave her a gentle shake. "Mrs. Bexley?"

She gasped, rising to a seated position and turning to gaze in confusion at Colin. "Oh. My apologies. I must have—"

"I'm sorry for the interruption to your sleep, but…" He looked pointedly at Hugh, and she followed his gaze.

"*No*," she breathed. Surging to her feet, she leaned forward and pressed the back of her hand to Hugh's forehead. "He has the fever."

* * *

Charlotte gripped a handful of flour and spread it over the kitchens' worktable, then placed the large, round piece of dough on top and began to knead. The safe house's kitchens were a great deal smaller than the one she'd had commissioned at her estate, but she didn't particularly care about the size at present.

Hugh had lain abovestairs for three days in the throes of his fever, and it was not to be borne. She'd scarcely left his side, but that morning, she required a bath and a distraction. Hugh's fellow spy Mary had been gracious enough to provide her the necessities in her bath, and now, she'd been in the kitchens for several hours, the light outside the kitchens' high window letting her know that it was already mid-afternoon.

Landing her fists in the dough, she gave it pound after pound, flattening it to the worktable's surface.

"Nae need te beat it into submission, Mrs. Bexley," Lord Winning said as he strode into the brightly lit kitchens.

Charlotte curled a stray lock of hair behind her ear and smiled sadly. "No, but it feels rather good."

He laughed, placing a pot of water on the hook above the hearth. "I certainly ken tha'. If ye've a need te punch something, however, there are dummies te pound in the training room."

"Thank you for the offer, Lord Winning, but I'd rather my punching have a purpose. And right now, that purpose is cheese buns."

He nodded as he withdrew some spices, bread, and meat from the larder. "I cannae complain. Yer cheese buns are fine, indeed."

"Thank you, Lord—"

"I'll nae have ye calling me 'Lord' anythin'. I'm Gabe." He smiled at her as he placed his burden on the other end of the worktable.

She felt warmed by his familiarity. He was one of Hugh's closest friends, and she rather enjoyed getting to know him better. "Very well, Gabe. And you must call me Charlotte."

His smile grew, and he laid out the items that he'd pulled from the larder.

"Excuse me, Mrs. Bexley." Mr. Greene strode through the door. "The Duke and Duchess of Norshire are here to see you. They're in the front parlour."

Charlotte's stomach jumped with nerves. "Thank you, Mr. Greene."

"I'll shape the buns, donnae ye worry." Gabe nodded to her.

With a muttered, "Thank you," she dusted her hands on a cloth and removed her apron, hanging them both on pegs near the door. With apprehension churning her insides and a quick nod to Gabe, Charlotte strode from the room and made her way toward the parlour.

It had been mere days since she'd seen the Duke, but the Duchess of Norshire had been absent from her life for nearly ten years, and their parting words had not been kind. His Grace assured Charlotte that she hadn't been exiled from her family as a result of her actions, but Papa had always been kinder-hearted than her mother.

She walked through the brightly lit corridors and the brilliance of the foyer to stand before the parlour's door. Her fingers trembling, she pressed the latch and swung the door wide.

Chapter 23

The moment Charlotte stepped over the threshold, the duchess rose to her feet and swept forward, tears misting her blue eyes as she pulled Charlotte into a tight embrace. First, confusion held Charlotte stiff. Years of believing that she'd been disowned by her family struggled against the waves of familial love that rode on her mother's tears.

After a brief pause, Charlotte returned her mother's hold, spreading her hands upon the older woman's back.

Charlotte's chest swelled, and heat pooled behind her stinging eyes. Her sudden reaction caught her unprepared, as the terror of the past days abruptly spilled forth. A sob rose up in her throat, and it escaped before she could suppress it.

She'd not known it before that moment, but an embrace from her mother was precisely what she'd needed.

Several moments passed before they parted. Charlotte wiped at her damp cheeks and looked more closely at her mother. Her Grace had aged in elegance. Her lips, forehead, neck, and chest were swathed in wrinkles, and her once-brown hair had very nearly turned white in its entirety. She stood regally, her head tall, her shoulders back, and her spine stiff. Precisely how Charlotte remembered her to be.

"Oh, my dear Charlotte," her mother whispered, dabbing with a finely embroidered handkerchief at a tear that perched on her lower eyelid. "We've missed you dreadfully."

The duchess reached out and wiped at Charlotte's chin, pulling her hand back to reveal flour on her fingertips. With a whispered, "Thank you," Charlotte wiped away the rest.

"I told your mother of our meeting," His Grace said, coming forward to stand beside his wife, his own eyes misted, "and of what you said to me."

Her Grace clasped Charlotte's hands in hers. "You must know, my darling, that your father and I never intended to push you away."

The ever-present ache in Charlotte's chest grew heavier. She didn't know what to say. She'd spent countless years believing that she'd been exiled, and now that she found she wasn't, Charlotte didn't particularly know where her place was.

She gave them a half smile. "Thank you. Shall I call for tea?"

The duchess returned Charlotte's smile with a big one of her own. "That would be lovely."

Her parents resumed their seats while Charlotte peered into the corridor to find one of the spies lurking there. She met a man's gaze and smiled. "How might one request tea?"

He returned her smile. "I shall see to it that a service is brought to you."

"Thank you."

She returned to the parlour.

"You look well," His Grace said as she sat on the settee across from them.

"Thank you." She nodded, smoothing out the skirts of her borrowed burgundy frock. "Tell me, how fares your search for Laura?"

Pain and sadness filled her parents' miens before her mother spoke. "We've searched for many weeks, and all of our inquiries have led us to the docks."

"We fear she was taken aboard a ship bound for the Americas," her father put in. "We have yet to learn any more than that. No one here seems to have seen her."

The last time that Charlotte had seen her younger sister, Laura was an impetuous and rebellious fourteen-year-old with wild, curling brown hair—very near to the shade of Charlotte's locks—and bright green eyes. Charlotte wondered what her sister would look like now.

"I'm sorry that your search has proved yet fruitless. I wish that I could be of help."

The duchess' reddened eyes misted once more. "Thank you, Charlotte, dear. While we're still grieving over your sister's disappearance, we're overjoyed to have *you* returned to us. I understand that we have grandsons!"

Speaking of her sons, Charlotte heard the faint shuffling of their knees and hands on the carpeted floor as they crept up behind her.

"I saw them only briefly on the journey here, but they do seem like sweet young boys," Papa said, reaching sideways to clasp Her Grace's hand in his. "We would be honoured, Charlotte, if you would allow us to renew our familial acquaintance."

"*Boo!*" Maximus jumped up from behind the settee, his arms held aloft and a large smile on his lips.

The duke and duchess showed genuine surprise, while Charlotte clutched her chest and gasped in feigned fright.

"My goodness, you frightened me!" Charlotte smiled at her four-year-old son, warmth spreading through her chest. She'd missed her sons dreadfully.

Quintin jumped up beside his brother and shouted, "I'm here, as well, Mama!"

"Oh my!" Charlotte grinned at him, then gestured for the boys to round the settee. "These are two people that I would like to introduce you to."

"Who are they, Mama?" Maximus came around to lean a forearm on her knees, while Quin jumped and sat beside her.

"This," Charlotte said, looking at her parents' swimming gazes, "is *my* mama and papa, the Duke and Duchess of Norshire." She added in an undertone to her sons, "You're to stand up straight—scoot off the settee—no slouching. Very good. Now, bow deeply."

The boys bowed in greeting, with Maximus bowing three additional times and jumping on his toes, with a flourish of his arms to complete the gesture.

Her parents laughed gaily, and Charlotte gestured to her sons.

"Mama, Papa, this is Quintin and Maximus Bexley."

"I'm Quin!" Quintin waved his hands.

"*And I'm Max!*" Maximus shouted, jumping on his toes once more. "I'm *four* years old, and Quin is seven! When I'm five, I'm going to lose my teeth. Would you like to hear me count to twenty?"

Her Grace beamed at the boys. "It is a pleasure to meet you both. I would very much enjoy listening to you count, Max."

"One, two—"

A knock sounded on the parlour's doorframe, and Charlotte turned from the warm moment to see Mary standing just inside the doorway, her eyes reddened. "I beg your pardon, Your Graces and Mrs. Bexley, but..." The woman squared her shoulders and pursed her lips. "We have need of Mrs. Bexley's presence abovestairs."

Her heart in her throat, Charlotte stood, setting her sons aside. "Hugh?" she breathed.

Mary nodded, her chin quivering.

A crushing weight landed upon Charlotte's chest, and despite her desire to dash immediately to Hugh's bedchamber, she turned to her parents. They'd stood, concern written upon their features.

"If you would not mind," her mother began, "we would be honoured if we could remain and spend some time with our grandsons."

"Mama told me about ices! Could we go for an ice?" Maximus asked loudly.

His Grace smiled down at her small son. "If we are given permission from your mama."

The four of them looked at Charlotte expectantly, and she nodded. "I would be very grateful if you would entertain the boys for as long as you wish."

"Fret not about your sons, darling," Her Grace said, putting a hand on Max's shoulder. "We will entertain them. See to your friend."

Charlotte's chest gave another hard squeeze, and with a hastily dipped curtsey, she departed.

"I say! Was that Miss Mary White?" His Grace's voice followed her through the foyer.

The moment they were out of sight of the parlour, Mary and Charlotte picked up their skirts and ran the distance to Hugh's bedchamber. They slowed before the door, entering at a sedate walk, and four pairs of sad eyes turned to gaze at her.

"What has happened?" she asked, stepping further into the room, her heart pounding against her ribs.

"His fever has worsened," Dr. Claridge replied. "In my experience, this is the most telling moment, whether the patient will survive or pass on. And I'm afraid that Hugh's condition does not inspire great hope." The doctor turned his gaze to the room at large. "My recommendation is for you to pay your respects. Say goodbye. Perhaps he will hear you and wish to fight. I would also recommend, Charles, that you summon Hugh's next of kin and a priest."

"Thank you, Simon," Hydra whispered before the two departed.

Undoubtedly, Sir Bradley was going to send word to Hugh's brother, Philip.

Hugh's rattling breath filled the room, and a great shuddering cough wracked his frame. Charlotte's heart clenched in a tight fist, her stomach dropping through to her toes.

Mary stepped forward first, gripped Hugh's pale hand in hers, and whispered to the dying man.

A sob caught in Charlotte's throat, and an arm slid over her shoulders. She looked up into Colin's red-rimmed brown eyes, tears streaming down his cheeks, and her control broke. With a great grimace, she wept. Uncontrollably and with startling intensity.

Colin's other arm encircled her, and she welcomed the embrace as her tears flowed. Her breaking heart shook her body with the force of its agony, spreading outward until her fingers trembled and her skin felt simultaneously tight and tingly.

Mary stood and swept quietly from the room before Gabe took her place at Hugh's bedside. The big man's shoulders shuddered as he whispered to Hugh. Colin's arms tightened around Charlotte, and hers around him.

Several moments passed before Gabe rose and turned tearfully to Colin and Charlotte. "It's your turn." He put a hand to Colin's shoulder.

Understanding her cue to withdraw, Charlotte released Hugh's friend and stepped back.

The two men shared a quick embrace and a pat on the back before Colin took his place beside Hugh, and Gabe stood solemnly at Charlotte's side. His hand slipped into hers and he gave it a gentle squeeze. She knew not if it was for encouragement or solidarity, but she appreciated the gesture nonetheless.

With a few more hushed words, Colin returned to Charlotte's side. "Would you like for us to remain with you?" he asked, his voice wavering and thick with grief.

Charlotte blinked, fighting to see through the tears swimming in her eyes, and whispered, "Thank you for your kindness, but no. I shall be fine." No, she wouldn't. But she had things to say that she did not wish for them to hear.

The men nodded and took their leave, and Charlotte sat on the chair beside Hugh's bed.

Even through the tears clouding her vision, she was still able to see the red of his cheeks against the sallowness of the rest of his exposed skin. She clasped his dry, hot hand in hers. His breathing was quick and shallow, and each of his faint coughs was followed by low groans.

"When I first saw you in that little outbuilding," she whispered, her voice wavering, "I didn't think that our time together would be like this. I didn't realize how eager I would be to see your face and hear your voice every day. You"—she sniffed—"you make me feel something that I've never before experienced.

"I can scarcely believe that it has been less than a sennight since I asked you to leave my kitchens. I ought not to have done that." She shook her head in self-reproach. "If you remained for but a few hours more, we would have been able to catch up to Reddington, and *this* mightn't have happened."

Hugh coughed and moaned, a deep frown puckering his pale brow.

Charlotte leaned forward and pressed her lips to the backs of his hot fingers. "Thank you. I see now how foolish I was for not trusting you. You are nothing like Mr. Bexley, but I believe that the more I became enamoured of you, the more my mind and sense of self-preservation urged me to distance myself.

"I understand why you withheld the truth from me, Hugh. I recognize and appreciate that you were trying to protect Quintin, Maximus, and me from potential harm. And I thank you for it. You risked—and possibly *gave*—your life to save my sons. I fear that there are not words strong enough to adequately express my appreciation."

Her tears dampened the bedclothes by their hands as she placed her forehead upon his fingers. She sniffled, the painful ache in her chest nigh more than she could bear. Her chest heaved with each sob.

"But…that is not why I have come to love you so deeply." She gasped before another cry escaped her. "I love you because you're kind, brave, and courageous. You're intelligent, comforting, caring…and you make me feel wanted and appreciated. But above all, you make my sons and me happy. Hugh, there are so many reasons for me to love you, but I've been blind to them until now. I wish…" Her throat thickened further, making her words come out in a squeaky whisper. "I wish that I could tell you that."

She pressed a kiss to his fingers once more, their heat warming her chilled skin.

"Please don't die, Hugh."

Chapter 24

"I am pleased that you've come, Philip." Colin shook Hugh's brother's roughened hand as the man strode into the safe house's darkened foyer.

The man nodded, his golden hair falling over his brow and his green eyes concerned. "I came as soon as I heard."

Colin took the man's coat, hat, and gloves. Philip Haddington looked very like Hugh in stature and colouring, though his hair was lighter, his green eyes were a mite darker, and his hands were slender and rough from working with gold all day.

"Would you care for some tea or coffee?" Colin asked.

"I thank you, no. May I see him?" His voice was low and hushed with grief.

"Of course. Right this way." Colin led the way up the stairs.

Philip cleared his throat. "What happened? Was he on assignment?"

Colin tilted his head in thought. "In a manner of speaking, yes. He'd been on assignment when he was captured. That was months ago, as you know, when he went missing. Mrs. Bexley—previously Lady Charlotte Morris—found Hugh in a diminutive outbuilding on Lord Reddington's land, tortured and near death—"

Philip halted mid-step in the corridor. "*Lord Reddington*?"

Turning to face him, Colin stopped, as well, and nodded. "Indeed. Mrs. Bexley took Hugh in and nursed him back to health. Angry, Reddington kidnapped the woman's sons, forcing Hugh and Mrs. Bexley to follow." His lips tightened in sorrow. "Hugh was shot from behind, and leapt into the River Thames with broken ribs to rescue the two young boys. We revived him on the boat, but the doctor has informed us that there is still water in Hugh's lungs."

Philip cursed, then followed Colin to Hugh's bedchamber. The room was dimly lit, but he could clearly see Charlotte's slumped form at the bedside. Her brown hair was mussed from laying her head on the bed's edge, and her back was crooked at an odd angle.

"Is that—?" Philip began.

Colin nodded. "Yes. That is Mrs. Bexley. She must be exhausted. I'll bring her to her chambers and allow you a moment alone with Hugh."

He strode forward on silent feet and carefully disentangled Charlotte's grip on Hugh's hand, lifting her in his arms and carrying her from the room. She curled into his chest, her eyes red and swollen, and Colin's heart squeezed. She was in pain, and would undoubtedly wish to remain at Hugh's side, but Colin knew that she would benefit from a full night of sleep, fitful though it would be.

Pushing her door open with the toe of his boot, he strode in, placed his burden on her bed, and pulled the coverlet up to her chin. The gesture reminded him of his sister, Isobel. He'd lost count of how many times he'd put her to bed after one of her tearful nights. It crushed him to think on it.

"Good night, Charlotte," he whispered before departing and closing the door behind him.

* * *

Hugh felt like death. His body pained him from the roots of his hair to the pads of his feet. He felt a brief moment of confusion before memories of the frigate and the water came flooding back.

Judging from the pain shooting through his side with each shallow breath, he'd been correct in his assumption that he'd broken a rib. He opened his eyes slowly, blinking against the brightness of the morning sunlight shining through the window that dominated the wall to his right.

Was it the morning after the incident at the frigate? How did the boys fare?

A gentle snore sounded beside him, and a smile spread across his lips. Had Charlotte joined him in bed? The stiffness in his neck notwithstanding, he turned to look to his right. Shock and mirth caught him off guard, and his smile grew. Lying beside him were Quintin and Maximus, their heads sharing the pillow next to Hugh's. Quin had curled into a ball against Max's side, while Max had spread his arms and legs out, stretching as far as his little limbs could go.

They both wore nightshirts and short pants that were far too long. Their small orange kitten curled against Maximus' ribs, purring slightly as he slept. Hugh laughed lightly, then cringed and groaned at the pain in his side.

Max's eyes snapped open, and his head popped up before he swivelled to face Hugh.

"Mr. Hugh!" The lad pushed at his older brother, waking him. "Mr. Hugh's awake!"

"Blimey!" Quin exclaimed.

Max shook his head at Quintin. "Mama says you should not say such words, Quin." He turned back to Hugh, absently stroking the kitten's fur. "You're not dead anymore!"

"I'm glad," Quin added.

"Me too." Max nodded.

Hugh opened his mouth to speak, but he croaked instead. He licked his lips. "I'm pleased to see you, as well, boys. I imagine your mama is glad to have you returned to her."

"She is," Quin confirmed. "We got to spend time with our grandpapa and grandmamma yesterday!"

"We had *ices*!" Max beamed at him. "They're *so* good! I could have eaten twenty."

"No, you couldn't," Quin protested. "Your mouth would have frozen right off."

"It would not!" Max put his fists on his waist and frowned at his brother, the movement frightening the kitten, who bounded off the bed and ran from the room.

"Where is your mama now?" Hugh asked, amused at the boys' antics and overjoyed to see them smiling once more. *Quite the change from yesterday.*

"When Miss Mary took us to bed, we saw Mr. Greene carrying Mama to her bedchamber. She's probably still sleeping." Quin shrugged one shoulder.

A faint swirling of jealousy wove through Hugh's gut, but he quickly squashed the feeling. Colin was merely performing a kind gesture, and—

A sharp gasp filled the bedchamber, followed by the *crash* and *clang* of a tray, laden with items, falling to the floor. Hugh turned his head toward the sound, his neck creaking as he did.

"*Hugh*," she breathed, her hands covering her mouth.

"Mama!" Max exclaimed. "Hugh's alive!"

Charlotte rushed forward, slowing only when she reached his bedside. "Oh, Hugh!" She placed the back of her hand to his forehead, and a sob escaped her.

"How do you feel?" she asked, hovering over him.

She stroked his forehead with her cool hand, and pleasure rolled through him. "I am well enough."

Tears misted her eyes before she pressed her lips to his in a quick buss.

The relief on her face sparked a moment of realization. "How long have I been lying here?"

"*Forever*," Quin said, dragging out the word.

"You died!" Max nodded.

"Oh, for pity's sake, boys. That's quite enough." Charlotte sent them a damp smile before turning back to Hugh. "You've been abed for just over four days."

"*Four* days?" His gut flipped over.

How close had he come to succumbing to his injuries? Hugh's heart swelled as he watched the joy play over Charlotte's features. She must truly have worried for him.

His realization from beneath the Thames wove through his thoughts as he gazed at her. He loved this woman. And, as uncertain as his future was, and as wrong as a duke's daughter was for him, he had to do right by his heart and *tell* her. Then, perhaps, he could have some semblance of hope for his future…

He reached for her hand and rubbed his thumb over her knuckles. "Before I forget, Charlotte, there is something that I'd meant to tell you—"

Heavy footfalls raced down the corridor, stopping at the opened door. "I heard a crash, and—" Hydra's gaze rose from the fallen tray and halted on Hugh. "By damn," he breathed before taking the two short steps to the bell pull and giving it a hard tug. At the safe house, the bell was reserved for emergencies or requests for aid, as they had no servants in residence—only spies.

Hugh flicked his tongue out to moisten his dry lips. "Was it as bad as all that, then?"

"You were only abed for a few days, Hugh, but you gave us quite the fright," Hydra said, striding forward. "I'm tremendously pleased to see that you've pulled through."

More heavy footfalls sped down the corridor. Within a heartbeat, Gabriel and Colin appeared, their complexions wan and worried.

Gabriel cursed soundly under his breath as he stared disbelievingly at Hugh.

"Mama," Maximus whispered, "Lord Winning said a curse word."

Charlotte nodded, her eyes misted. "Gabe is an adult, and is allowed to use whatever language he chooses."

"I've a mind to punch you in the teeth for making us worry over your damned hide," Colin said, grinning. "I'm bloody glad that you're awake."

"How do ye feel?" Gabe asked Hugh.

"Like death," Hugh answered truthfully. "But I'm pleased to see all of you. Gabriel, you've got a little something on your face." He smirked at his friend as he eyed the long scar running down the side of Gabe's temple and along his jaw.

"Bastard." Gabe grinned in return.

Quick footsteps sounded just outside the door, preceding the entrance of Dr. Claridge, Mary Wright, and...

Shock rippled through Hugh. "*Philip*? What the devil are you doing here? I'm right pleased to see you, but—"

"I summoned him," Hydra put in.

His fair brother stood next to Charlotte at his bedside, his eyes reddened. "You were at death's door. Of course I came to see you."

Hugh turned his surprised gaze on the doctor, who nodded. "In my experience, only a very small number of patients who survive drowning and still have water in their lungs live through the fever, most particularly those whose ribs are broken. You not only defied those odds, but you also suffered with the other injuries that you sustained over the past months." Dr. Claridge cleared his throat. "It is my recommendation that you remain abed with little excitement or movement for another fortnight, at least."

Another wave of shock crashed through Hugh. The doctor's list of injuries explained the agony searing through him. And Christ, but he'd not been aware of any of the past few days.

A cough caught him by surprise, and a jolt of pain went across his ribs. He grimaced.

"I daresay that having the lot of us in Hugh's bedchamber is more excitement than he needs," Hydra murmured.

"Thank you—all of you—for your concern and your aid," Hugh said to the group. "I would very much like to speak with all of you, but perhaps I might have a word with Philip first?"

"Come, boys." Charlotte moved to the foot of the bed and reached a hand to her sons. "Let us leave Hugh to a discussion with his brother." She smiled at Hugh over her shoulder as the boys clambered from the bed.

"Of course." Hydra nodded. "We are very pleased to have you back with us."

The others murmured their agreement and smiled at him as they filed out, leaving Philip and Hugh alone in the bedchamber.

Philip sat in the chair at his side. "I'm glad that you are well, brother. It's been far too long since I've seen you. We've been very worried."

"I apologize for your distress."

"I'm sorry for *yours*." Philip shook his head. "I can scarcely countenance what you must have suffered…"

Memories of his time in Reddington's hold threatened to play themselves over in his mind, but Hugh pushed them away. "How fares Emma and the children?"

His brother smiled wistfully at the mention of his wife. "They are well, indeed. Bernard celebrated his sixth birthday just last month and will not cease talking about it. Ruby is two and causes all sorts of mischief."

"I miss them dreadfully," Hugh admitted. "And Emma?"

Philip beamed. "Expecting our third, actually. And very well. She will enter her confinement in a few months."

Hugh wanted that. He wanted a wife and children; he wanted a *future*…with Charlotte.

He cleared his throat. "My felicitations, brother."

"My thanks. Now, what of you? Have you—"

Nerves fluttered in his stomach as instinct and impulse took hold. "Actually, there is a favour that I must ask of you."

Philip inclined his head. "Anything."

"I have need of your services…"

Chapter 25

Days slipped by for Hugh as he lay abed. He was gathering his strength, and soon he would be able to sit up to converse with his fellows and Charlotte. For the moment, however…

"I'll be the dragon this time!" Maximus shouted.

Quin groaned loudly. "Fine. But I get to be it next time. I'll be the knight, and Jack can be my squire!"

"Oh, but I wanted Jack to be my baby dragon," Max complained.

"If you get to be the dragon, *I* get Jack."

"Very well. Now, run!"

There was a squeal and swift footfalls running about Hugh's bedchamber.

"I'm going to burn the village down," Max threatened in an affected deep voice.

"Beware my sword!" Quin squealed.

Hugh smiled at the ceiling as the boys continued to play. He and Philip had played like that when they were young.

Being around the boys was a balm to his troubled soul. And, truthfully, he didn't like the thought of being apart from them and Charlotte again. What could he do to entice her to stay? Hugh had nothing tangible to offer.

He'd failed at spying, and was entirely unfit to be in the field—no matter how much he might desire it. He could teach at Grimsbury Manor, but who would wish for *him* to teach the future generation of spies? He, who had clearly lost his abilities?

Philip might hire him, should Hugh ask. The jewellery business, however, held no excitement or intrigue, and though it would provide an income, Hugh could not imagine doing such staid work.

A sigh escaped him, which led to a cough that burned in his chest and clenched the already-sore muscles in his back, shoulders, and abdomen. Hell, but he was very nearly entirely useless.

He was certainly not enough to entice the daughter of a duke.

Dramatic cries of agony erupted from beyond the foot of Hugh's bed, and for the briefest of moments, concern washed over him. Until, of course, he realized what has happened.

"You've killed me!" Maximus moaned. "Struck through the heart by my very own *brother*!"

"But, dragon! I did not know that you were my brother, cursed by the evil sorceress whom you'd scorned!"

Oh, delightful twist, Hugh mused.

Soft footfalls came from the corridor, followed by a light *tsk*.

"Have a care, boys," Charlotte said. "Hugh must recover in peace. You mustn't jostle him."

Her beautiful face appeared in his line of sight, and he smiled up at her. "Good day, Mrs. Bexley."

She returned his smile, her eyes warm and crinkling in the corners. Damn, but he loved the woman. He'd wanted to tell her so before, but something was missing between them. *The truth* was missing between them. He'd spent so much time fabricating a life that he worried she wouldn't know who he truly was. He aimed to change that.

* * *

"I miss your buttons," Hugh said, catching Charlotte's gaze across the coverlet and sending her a wink.

Her pulse sped, and, not for the first time in the past days, her mind strayed to what Hugh had said when he'd first awoken after his fever: *Before I forget, Charlotte, there is something that I'd meant to tell you.* But *what* had he meant to tell her? She'd thought to ask him but didn't wish to press him. When he felt the moment was right, he would speak his mind.

"The card is yours." Charlotte handed him the ten of hearts and flipped over the next card. "Now, you were telling me about your school for spies."

Hugh grinned at her, his back propped against a plethora of pillows. "The cook in Grimsbury Manor taught all of us to prepare food. Some took to it, while others learned how to feed themselves some simple fare and then focused their attention on their other subjects."

Charlotte lifted one eyebrow. "I assume that you were in the latter group of students?"

"Of course. My favourite courses were tailing and pistols."

"Mmm," she hummed, nodding. "And what did you favour when you were a child? Did they teach little ones the same courses?"

He shrugged one shoulder. "At that age, I did whatever Philip would do. We'd lost our parents, and I feared so much that I would lose him, as well, that I followed him everywhere. He despised it, of course."

She nodded, awareness dawning. "So you began to follow him in secret."

His lips quirked. "Yes."

He slid a small torn piece of parchment across the coverlet. "My wager."

"No." She shook her head. "Too small."

His gaze sharpened on hers, then darkened. "I will wager you one kiss."

With a twist of her lips, she feigned deep thought. "Very well, I accept. Turn over your cards."

They revealed their cards and, alas, the trick was hers.

* * *

His heart racing and his nerves on edge after his visit with Philip that morning, Hugh tapped his fingers on the coverlet as he spoke with his superior.

"Did the visit with your brother conclude satisfactorily?" Hydra asked from his seat at his bedside.

A smile spread across Hugh's lips. "Indeed, it did." He eyed his superior with curiosity. "I've been meaning to inquire after your wife…"

Hydra's eyes glazed over and a slow, secretive grin stole over his features at the mention of his wife. "Bridget is well. *Very* well."

"And she is accepting of your life in the Secret Service?"

"Accepting? Lord, no. Bridget does not merely accept my position with the Home Office, she endorses it. In fact, she's been hinting that she'd like to join me, now that the war is over."

Mirth crept through Hugh. That certainly sounded like Lady Bridget Bradley. "And will you have her join you?"

Hydra shrugged one shoulder. "She *is* the most proficient swordswoman I've ever met—"

"I heard that she bested *you*, sir."

His superior cut him a withering glance. "Stubble it."

Hugh laughed, then cringed at the ache in his side.

"What of you?" Hydra asked. "Dr. Claridge says it might be above four weeks before you are fully recovered and ready to return to the field. The war is over, but the Secret Service will always require men." He paused, but spoke before Hugh could reply. "Of course, there are other options. I believe that Gabe and Mary have decided to teach at Grimsbury Manor, and, as you know, there is a discussion among several of the men to branch out into Bow Street Running."

Hugh's chest ached and his stomach knotted as he gazed at his expectant superior. He'd known that this moment would come, and he detested it. "My skills as a tail…" He trailed off, uncertainty and self-loathing swamping him as he remembered the night he was taken by Reddington. "I am…not what I once was."

A swift frown spread across Hydra's brow. "Your *skills*—" All at once, his eyes widened and shock lined his features. He leaned forward to rest his elbows on his knees. "Hugh, are you under the assumption that it was your lack of skill that caused your capture?"

Hugh was taken aback by the question. "Of course! Reddington knew I was following him because my—"

"No! No, no." Hydra shook his head. "Hugh, there was a leak. One of Napoleon Bonaparte's spies infiltrated our system and turned two of my men to their cause. Your name was *given* to Reddington, as were Barrows', Samuels', and Callum's. *You* are not responsible for your capture. *I* am."

The words hung in the air between them, and a glimmer of hope sparked in Hugh's chest. Had he truly been labouring under a misapprehension for the past months? Had he truly accepted Reddington's torture and prepared himself for death under the assumption that *he* was at fault for failing and being caught?

Putting his elbow on the window's sill, Hugh rubbed at his lips with the backs of his fingers as his pulse sped. *It wasn't my fault.* That changed his plans for the future somewhat. *What will Charlotte think?* He could scarcely wait to tell her.

* * *

The alluring scent of spices, vegetables, and tender beef swirled around Charlotte's nose as she stirred the enormous simmering pot over the fire in the kitchens. Her mouth watered, and a smile played over her lips.

Quick, light footfalls crept up behind her, and Charlotte braced for what she knew was to come.

"*Boo!*" Max giggled, and Charlotte spun around in mock surprise.

"Oh, my heavens, Maximus!"

"I scared you, Mama!" he exclaimed, a broad smile on his lips.

Charlotte nodded. "Indeed, you did."

Mary sped into the kitchens with Quintin at her side. "Good morning, Charlotte. My, it smells wonderful in here."

"Mama makes the *best* beef stew," Quin noted.

Charlotte laughed. "It's hardly the best, but I thank you, nonetheless."

"I'm sure it will be divine." Mary nodded as Quin slipped his hand in hers. "I'd thought to take the boys into the gardens for some theatrical play."

"We're going to prepare a performance!" Maximus shouted, bouncing on his toes.

"That sounds lovely." Charlotte turned a stern eye on the boys. "Be sure to listen to Mary's instructions and play safe, you two."

"We will, Mama," the boys said in unison.

With a smile and a wave, the boys tromped from the room with Mary following close behind. Charlotte grinned and turned to the worktable, spreading flour across its surface. She removed the cloth from the bowl in which her crumpet dough had been rising, and dumped the contents upon the floured worktable.

The demand for aid in the kitchens had increased over the past days, for the two gentlemen who had retreated to Charlotte's home, Mr. McCully and Mr. Thomson, had ventured to London once Thomson had been well enough to travel. The poor man had an awful scar as a result of his knife wound. She hardly knew how to thank him for saving her life such as he did. Baking for everyone was the least that she could do.

Early morning sun shone through the kitchens' opened window, and a bird sang somewhere beyond. She sank her palms into the dough and kneaded it.

"Nae punching th' dough any longer, I see." Gabe strode into the kitchens with an empty silver salver.

Charlotte laughed. "Indeed not."

With a grin, Gabe notched his chin toward the pot above the hearth. "Is tha' the stew fer luncheon?"

"Yes, and these will be the buns to accompany it."

"Verra good. I believe that the boys are preparing a performance, if you've a mind te watch."

A grin stole over her features, and joy leapt in her heart. "Certainly."

"I'll take over th' forming of th' buns, Charlotte. Enjoy."

Chapter 26

"A…alas, my sword shall… What am I supposed to say?" Quintin held a stick high in the air, a look of confusion on his features as he turned to Mary for help in their rehearsal.

Charlotte fanned herself with one of Mary's elaborately painted fans, her heart full of pride as she watched her sons rehearsing. They were charming and adorable. Maximus lowered himself to his hands and knees and pretended to be the knight's noble steed, then giggled when the small kitten, Jack, rubbed against his arm. It shocked Charlotte every day how very much she loved them.

The boys ran around in a circle, the knight comically chasing his mount. Laughter bubbled up in Charlotte's chest. Lord, but laughter was a fine thing. How long had it been since she'd truly laughed?

The midmorning sun shone brightly, rising in the sky from the east with nary a cloud to block its light. It was warm but not hot, drying the water from the rainy days before.

A hand covered her shoulder, and Charlotte jumped, spinning in her chair on the grass.

"Hugh!" She moved to stand, but he halted her.

"It's quite all right," he rumbled, placing a chair at her side.

He sat with a great sigh. The arm of his chair was pressed against hers, forcing their forearms to touch. Her stomach bunched with nerves as he clasped her hand in his. It was a forward and familiar gesture, but she cared not who saw. Hugh was alive, and she would appreciate any moment that she had with him.

They watched the boys in companionable silence.

Quin waved his "sword" in the air while Max galloped around the grass, the kitten chasing after them. The boys were growing so quickly. Charlotte knew not where the years had gone.

"Mr. Bexley never knew that I was *enceinte* with Maximus before he died," she confessed aloud.

Hugh turned his gaze to her profile and squeezed her hand encouragingly.

"Indeed," she continued, "I was afraid to tell him, for after Quintin was born, Mr. Bexley spent fewer and fewer hours at home, leaving me alone with the baby. He made excuses about his absences. I believed him because I loved him."

Maximus roared. "I'm a dragon now! I'm going to get you!"

Quin screeched and ran away, with Max and Mary chasing after him. They ran about for several moments before they turned toward Charlotte.

"Mama! Mr. Hugh!" the boys called to them as they ran over.

Charlotte's stomach jumped. "Remember Hugh's injuries!"

The boys skidded to a halt before them, and Charlotte sighed a breath of relief.

"We're rehearsing a play," Quintin announced. "It will be ready for us to perform on the morrow."

"*I'm a horse!*" Max screeched, jumping with his arms lifted straight above his head.

"How fascinating." Hugh smiled at them both. "I am very much looking forward to seeing your performance. In fact, I would love to continue watching you rehearse, but I find myself rather tired. Would you excuse me?"

"Yes!" Maximus jumped again.

He turned to Charlotte. "Would you be so kind as to aid me?"

* * *

A dull ache had settled into Hugh's ribs, but the last thing that he wanted to do was *rest*.

The moment they entered his bedchamber, Charlotte hurried to the tray of food that sat upon the table.

"The morning meal is still edible, if you do not mind it being slightly cool, but the coffee is just dreadful. I will go to the kitchens and refresh the—"

Snick. The sound of the lock sliding into place filled the room, and Charlotte spun to face him. Hugh stepped forward and pulled the coat from his shoulders, tossing it to one of the table's chairs. He knew that the desire on his features would be unmistakable, for hell if he couldn't go one more day without having her, injuries or not.

Charlotte's gaze turned quickly from a mixture of curiosity and concern to longing. It fired his blood. He stepped forward again, untying his cravat.

"Hugh," she said in a warning tone. "You know full well that your wounds require time to heal. Why, your ribs alo—"

"My ribs ache, but they will not stop me from enjoying myself, as long as I am careful." He took the final step toward her, slipping one hand along the side of her jaw so the tips of his fingers touched the silken brown hair that she'd pulled into a knot, and his thumb caressed her cheek. "There is something that I've been meaning to tell you, Charlotte," he whispered.

Her eyes closed on a sigh before opening once more, bright blue and misted. "I've been waiting to hear the end of that thought," she whispered in return. "I began to wonder if I'd ever hear it."

Hugh's stomach quivered with nerves and suppressed desire, and a grin tugged at his lips. "I apologize for the suspense." His gaze turned solemn. "You are an extraordinary woman. You handle strife with composure, you are independent, brave, kind, courageous, strong, and above all else, you are a wonderful mother to two exceptional boys." He paused, gazing deeply into her swimming eyes and stroking her soft cheek with the pad of his roughened thumb. "I love you, Charlotte."

Her face crumpled, tears leaking from her tightly squeezed eyelids, and Hugh's heart gave a hard thump. She cupped his jaw in her hands and lifted on her toes to press her lips to his in an ardent kiss. He tasted the salt of her tears and the lingering sweetness of her morning tea.

She pulled back to look into his eyes, her nose a hair's breath away from his. "I love you too, Hugh."

His heart soared at those five little words, and with a growl of satisfaction, he pressed a passionate kiss to her waiting lips. She sighed, wrapping her arms around his shoulders and raking her fingers in his hair. Tingles skittered along his scalp and down his spine, tugging at his cods and urging blood to his cock.

With his hands on her hips, Hugh walked Charlotte backward toward the bed. Her thighs touched the edge, and she reclined. Bending to grip her hem, he lifted the material of her borrowed frock, petticoats, and chemise up over her legs to bunch around her waist. With a wink to her, Hugh knelt on the floor and spread her thighs wide, his gaze feasting on her folds, ripe for his delectation.

"Hugh, what are you—"

"Merely repaying the favour, love." He grinned at her before leaning forward and testing her readiness with the tip of his tongue.

Charlotte gasped, and his erection gave a responding throb.

Using his fingers to spread her open, Hugh swirled his tongue over her pearl. Her moans and gasps urged him on, and further aroused him. He pressed his tongue harder and moved faster, until she was writhing.

His cock strained his falls and his heart pumped a staccato beat in his chest as her moans seeped into him. He wanted her to have more, to feel more. Moving his hold to her hips to keep her still, he redoubled his efforts.

Abruptly, her back arched, and a keening cry filled his ears. He could scarcely keep his eyes from rolling backward as he stood, wiping at his mouth with the back of his shirtsleeve. His eagerness to be inside her was nigh too much to bear.

He wrestled with the fall of his trousers, until he finally sprang free. Hugh bent over Charlotte, placing one hand at her shoulder as his other guided his erection into her soft, wet passage.

"Oh, Hugh," she moaned, reaching for his shoulders.

He groaned as he sheathed himself fully inside her. His skin felt tight, his heart raced, but he held himself still, enjoying the moment of being in Charlotte.

His feet still on the floor, he put his elbows to the mussed coverlet and kissed her. "I love you," he whispered against her lips.

She smiled. "I love you, too."

Then, he started to move. Slowly at first, then with increased fervour.

"You…inflame me…Charlotte."

A sweat broke out across his brow as he pumped faster. His ribs ached, but he didn't want to stop.

"Hugh!" Charlotte gasped, clutching his hair and wrapping her legs around his hips.

He thrust hard and fast, holding off on his own completion until Charlotte found hers once more. And then, it happened.

Her jaw dropped open on a silent cry, and her head pressed back into the bed, her sheath pulsing around him.

It sent him over the edge after her. With one last pump, he moved to withdraw, but Charlotte's heels dug into his rear, holding him.

"I love you," she whispered.

His heart squeezed, and, with a roar, Hugh bared his teeth and came, spilling his seed deep inside her.

Chapter 27

It was immensely satisfying to watch Hugh come apart. His teeth were bared, his brows turned upward in an expression of helplessness, and the veins in his neck and forehead bulged. Charlotte liked it very much.

With a great sigh, Hugh slumped forward, their racing hearts pressed against each other. They lay thusly for several long moments, their breath slowing as she stroked his soft hair.

Charlotte closed her eyes, content to remain there with Hugh in her arms.

He sniffed, and rose up on his elbows to look her in the eyes.

"I came inside you," he said, his voice low.

"I know."

His features were carefully blank. "You do not mind—"

Charlotte put her hands to his cheeks. "I love you, Hugh. I would be honoured to have a child with you, should it happen one day."

To her astonishment, tears formed in his eyes then spilled over his lashes, dripping onto her wrinkled bodice.

"Oh, Hugh." She rose to a seated position, forcing Hugh to stand and re-fasten his trousers. She kissed his cheek and wrapped her arms about his shoulders in a comforting embrace.

He swiped at his cheeks and sniffed. "I'd not thought it possible, finding love."

"I understand the feeling."

"What of my position in the Secret Service?"

"I'm not certain that I understand the question." She frowned in puzzlement. "What of it?"

"If I took assignments, I would be forced to leave you and the children."

"But you would come back?" she asked, already knowing his answer.

"Of course. Though I understand that there are other options for me now that the war is over."

She pulled back to look into his reddened green eyes. "I trust you, Hugh. Whatever you decide, I will be here to support you."

He sniffed again and pressed his face into the crook of her neck. "Thank you." His voice was muffled. It was a few moments more before she heard him mumble something else, but she couldn't quite make it out.

"I beg your pardon?" she asked before he lowered himself to kneel on one knee, and she spotted the item held between his forefinger and thumb. Her eyes widened at the breathtakingly beautiful ring. A large diamond sat affixed to the middle of a startlingly pink-tinted gold band with smaller diamonds on either side.

"I cannot offer you a title or land, but I can offer my heart, my companionship, and my life. Charlotte, my Angel, would you do me the great honour of becoming my wife?"

Her breath caught in her throat and her eyes grew watery. "Yes, of course!"

* * *

There was no other feeling in the world like proposing to the woman he loved and having her say yes. Not many men and women could say that they'd ever *been* in love; Hugh felt exceedingly fortunate to have such a connection. And to The Angel, of all women.

His chest swelled with pride, but his stomach buzzed with nerves as he stood in the parlour awaiting the arrival of Quintin and Maximus. He'd gained consent from Charlotte, but now he must do so with her sons.

Quick, light footsteps came down the corridor, preceding the bouncing entrance of the two boys. Hugh grinned at them, though his stomach flipped over.

"Mr. Hugh!" Max hopped forward.

"Maximus. Quintin." He inclined his head, then gestured toward the settee. "Please be seated."

They both sat, and Hugh took the chair nearest to them, perching on the edge with his elbows resting on his knees.

"I think that you both are bright, enjoyable, and kind young men with many admirable qualities."

"Thank you!" Quin bounced in his seat. "I think so, too."

"Yeah, me, too!" Max beamed.

Hugh's chuckle eased the nerves humming in his abdomen. "I love your mother, and wish to—"

Maximus gasped, leaping to his feet. "Are you going to be our papa?"

Hugh smiled at the boys. "I'd very much hoped so, yes. But only if it is al—"

"*Yes!*" Max screeched, his fists high in the air. "I get a papa!"

Quintin bounced off the couch and rushed to Hugh, wrapping his arms tightly around Hugh's neck. "I'm so glad that we get to keep you."

Warmth spread through Hugh's chest, and the backs of his eyes tingled. "I am, as well." He was, rather more than he ever thought he could be.

Maximus joined their embrace, wrapping his arms around Hugh and Quin. "I always wanted a papa."

Hugh's heart gave another hard thump, and the prickling in his eyelids grew stronger. Never would he have thought that he would not only fall in love with Charlotte, but that he could also hold enough love in his heart for two sweet boys, as well.

Epilogue

A fortnight later

Charlotte sipped at her champagne as she strode arm in arm with her new husband about the grand parlour at Grimsbury Manor, surrounded by her parents and Hugh's fellow spies at their wedding breakfast. They could not wait to marry, and had foregone posting the banns—with her father's help, naturally.

Her sons were dashing in their suits, regardless of the smattering of orange fur that covered them. And her husband… She turned her gaze up to Hugh's profile, and her stomach fluttered. She loved him more with every passing moment.

A quiet midsummer rain fell beyond the brightness coming in the windows, making her feel rather content to be indoors.

"Oh! My dear Charlotte!" Her Grace stepped before them, halting their walkabout, and pulled them both into her familial embrace. "And handsome Hugh! Oh, you've both made me so happy today. You will have a long and joyous marriage, I am absolutely certain."

"Thank you, Mama."

A commotion sounded at the entrance, and they spun toward the source. Mr. Brown entered, his mien harried and his clothes sopping. His gaze scanned the crowd until he found Sir Charles Bradley, who stood near Hugh and Charlotte with his wife, Bridget, on his arm.

"Hydra!" the man called as he hurried forward.

"Brown!" Hydra frowned. "What in God's name has you so weary? Were you not in London?"

"I rode from town as quickly as I could." The man huffed an exhausted breath. "I have news from Callum and Harris. They sent word on a ship bound for London that they encountered—"

"I don't care how the letter came to us, Brown. What did it *say*?"

Brown, discomfited, shifted his gaze to the guests around them, then returned it to his superior. "They've found the Duke of Norshire's daughter Lady Laura Morris."

www.ingramcontent.com/pod-product-compliance
Lightning Source LLC
Chambersburg PA
CBHW021146190726

48288CB00008B/2851